The Rock

Barney Alesi

Dedication

I am dedicating this book to my wife, Rose, also known as my sweetheart, love of my life, and soul mate, because she put up with me bemoaning about the book and with all the hours and hours on end of being alone while I was in my man cave working on this book

Acknowledgments

I want to give special thanks to several people who made it possible for me to write this book: Rose Alesi, my wife, who put up with me and listened to me for hours and hours on end as I complained about all of the problems I encountered while writing this book; my nephew Michael Santo, Esq., my two daughters, Bonnie and Theresa, along with my son, Anthony, my grandchildren, Anthony, Tiffany, Jacqueline, Nicholas, Kaitlynn, and Patrick; my daughters-in-law, Sue and Denise, my granddaughter-in-law, Kati, and grandson-in-law, Sal. I also want to thank my friends, who have listened to me moaning about my book and who deserve to at least be recognized: Bob, Maryann, Jimmy, Nick, Janet, John, Celeste, James, and Barb.

Contents

LIFE IS GOOD

Billy Johnson is just a normal twelve-year-old boy who lives with his mother, Mary, and father, Jake, in a modest two-bedroom house on Long Island, NY. Jake drives a bus for a living, and Mary works part time in the school's cafeteria, and they live a very normal lifestyle.

Billy is a very active young boy who loves to play basketball, baseball, and hockey, and one of the things he loves the most is riding his bike, which he calls Phil. It is never out of his sight unless he is sleeping. The biggest dream that Billy has, though, is to one day become an astronaut and fly to Mars, and his room shows it. He has pictures of every astronaut on his walls and plastic models of all the rockets that NASA has used. He has pictures of the universe and the solar system and a blowup picture of the Milky Way on his walls. If it has anything to do with space travel, Billy will have it in his room. In fact, this year for Halloween, he bought a spacesuit costume to wear for trick or treating.

Life is going well for the Johnson family. They are just

an all-around happy family until, one day, the unthinkable happens. Billy and a group of his friends are at the base-ball field, choosing up sides for a baseball game, when, all of a sudden, they hear tires screeching, and as they look toward the sound, they see a large SUV breaking through the chain-link fence and heading straight toward them. Filled with fear, they cannot move a muscle, and the SUV plows right into them. The boys go flying in all directions, and the SUV just keeps on going, not even hinting that it might stop. In fact, the driver even speeds up to get away. Thankfully someone in the ballpark saw what happened and calls for an ambulance and the police.

In the meantime, other people in the park run over to see what they can do. The young boys are spread out all over the place. There are seven of them on the ground, some still moving, some unconscious. Unfortunately, none of the people trying to help know any first aid, so all they can do is to try to comfort them. Some of the women are crying, some are cursing out the driver, and some are asking, "How could anyone do something like this and just drive away without a care in the world?" It is just chaos, with people running around trying to help but accomplishing nothing but adding to the chaos.

Suddenly, they can hear sirens in the distance. "Oh, thank God! They're coming!" someone shouts.

Two police cars and one ambulance pull up. As soon as they stop, one of the policeman jumps out of his car, quickly assesses the situation, and says, "We are going to need more ambulances." He counts all the children and immediately gets on the radio and calls for six more ambulances.

While waiting for the additional ambulances to arrive, the two medics from the one that is already there start checking on all the boys. They go first to the ones who are not moving and quickly realize that they are unconscious and cannot speak for themselves. Then the medics assess the boys' injuries, and after concluding that they've just had the wind knocked out of them, the medics check out the rest of the boys. It seems the injuries range from cuts and bruises to broken bones and possibly some concussions, but the medics are especially concerned with two of the boys: Billy and his friend Tom. Both boys seem okay, aside from Billy having a broken arm and some cuts and bruises, but they are both complaining that they cannot feel or move their legs, which is a concern to the medics.

At this point, the other ambulances show up, bringing the total to seven. The boys are evaluated, put in the ambulances, and taken to nearby hospitals. Billy, Tom, and one other boy go to St. Catherine's Hospital in Smithtown, NY, and the other four go to Southside Hospital in Bay Shore, NY. Before they leave, though, the police question them to get information as to where they live, their phone numbers, etc. so that they can contact the boys' families to let them know what is going on. By then, more police cars have arrived, and while the ambulances head to the hospitals, the policemen, who have been given all the information they need, also leave to inform each individual family.

Back home at the Johnsons, Mary is busy preparing dinner when the doorbell rings. As she walks to the door, the top half of which is made of glass, she can't help but notice that it's a policeman, and she gets a knot in her stomach. Nervously, she opens the door and says, "Yes,

Officer, can I help you?"

"Are you Mrs. Johnson?"

"Yes, why are you asking who I am? What is wrong?"

"Mrs. Johnson, I have some bad news for you. It seems that your son Billy was struck by a car and was taken to the hospital."

"Oh my God!" shouts Mary. "Is he okay? And when did this happen?"

"It happened about an hour ago, and he was taken to St. Catherine's hospital in Smithtown. If you don't have any means of getting there, I can drive you if you want."

"Okay, officer, thank you. Just let me shut off the stove and oven. I was in the middle of preparing dinner." With that, Mary runs back inside, turns the stove and oven off, grabs her coat, and runs out the door, all the while shouting, "Oh my God! How could something like this happen?"

Asking the policeman to please hurry, Mary and the officer get into the police car and head toward the hospital. Halfway there, she realizes she forgot her cell phone at home.

The officer says, "Not to worry. You can use my phone."

Mary takes his phone and calls the office of the bus company where her husband works. She explains the situation to them and asks if they could please try to get in touch with her husband so that he can meet her up at the hospital. Nervously, she starts questioning the policeman.

"Can you tell me any more about what happened?"

"No, I'm sorry. The only information we had was that a large, black SUV careened off the road and crashed through a fence and ran over a group of young boys. It did not stop and sped off. There were several people in the park, but none of them got a plate number. As far as I know, your son was conscious, with some cuts and bruises. Other than that, you're going to have to wait to get the hospital to find out more about his injuries."

With that, they pull up to the hospital's emergency room entrance. Mary jumps out of the car before it even comes to a full stop and runs into the emergency room, frantically looking for her son and asking the nurse behind the counter,

"Where is Billy Johnson? I'm his mother, and I want to see him!"

"Okay, please wait a moment, and I'll check."

The nurse picks up the phone and asks the person who answers, "Do you have a Mr. Billy Johnson back there? His mother is here to see him. Okay thank you." She hangs up the phone and says, "Mrs. Johnson, someone will be right out to escort you in to see your son."

With that, another nurse comes out and says, "Mrs. Johnson, please follow me."

The nurse escorts Mary back into the emergency room, where Billy is. He is on a gurney in a little cubicle separated from the others by just a curtain. Mary runs over to him and tries to hug and kiss him to sort of comfort him, but there are so many things hooked up to him that she can't find an easy access, so she grabs the one free hand that he has and caresses and kisses it, asking, "Billy, what did you do? How did this happen? Are you in any pain?"

"No, Mom, I'm not in any pain. They gave me a shot, and I don't remember how it happened. All I know is we were choosing up sides for the game when, all of a sudden,

I heard screeching tires and saw a big, black car coming toward us, and the next thing I know I was being put in an ambulance. But Mom, I can't feel or move my legs."

Mary shouts out, "What!!"

Just then, a nurse is passing the cubicle. Mary stops her and asks if she could get a doctor to come and speak with her.

"Okay, ma'am. The doctor is busy right now, but if you want, that is him right over there, sitting at that desk. It would be a lot faster if you went to talk to him rather than wait for him to come to you."

"Okay, thank you."

Mary tells Billy, "I'm going to go over and talk to the doctor. I will be right back."

She walks over to where the doctor is sitting at the desk and says, "Excuse me, Doctor."

"Yes, can I help you?"

"I hope so. I'm Mrs. Johnson, and I understand that you're my son's doctor. I wanted to talk to you about his condition, about him not feeling or being able to move his legs."

"I am extremely concerned about that, Mrs. Johnson. It is a little too early to give a diagnostic evaluation. We need to get him upstairs to get an x-ray of his arm and back before we do anything else. As soon as we can, we will get him up there, and after reviewing it, then I will be able to give you more specific information. Until then, though, I cannot give you any information, because I don't know the extent of his injuries. I know you're upset and don't want to hear this, but please give us a little more time to evaluate him."

"Okay, thank you, Doctor, but it's just that I am really concerned."

"Mrs. Johnson, I completely understand where you're coming from. If it were my child, I would be feeling exactly the same way. I will call x-ray now and find out what the holdup is and try to have them speed up the process a little."

"Okay thank you, Doctor. I will wait until you have more information for me."

Mary then goes back to her son's side. Ten minutes later, two young men show up and explain to Mary that they are taking Billy up to x-ray, and if she could please wait in the waiting room, they will notify her when they return with him. Forty minutes later, the doctor comes into the waiting room to speak to her.

"Mrs. Johnson, first let me say this. Right now, he is okay, and I don't want you to worry. You know what they say, no news is good news, so I have to tell you that he does have a broken arm and right now they are putting a cast on it. As far as the cut on his forehead, they were able to take care of that without stitches. Now, as far as his legs go, I looked at the x-ray, and I cannot tell too much from it. Right now, it looks like there is no reason that he can't move or feel his legs, but I am scheduling an MRI for him in the morning, and I will have an expert, Dr. Philips, take a look at the results. He will be able to tell us exactly what's going on. So, until then, hope for the best and prepare for the worst. As soon as they finish with his cast, they will bring him down and let you know that he's back so that you can go be with him."

"Okay, Doctor, I'll wait here until they come and get

me. Thank you."

Just then, she hears Jake's voice asking about Billy. She walks over to him. "Jake, I'm over here."

"Where is he, and how is he, and how in the hell did this happen?"

"Evidently, he was at the school's baseball field with a group of boys, choosing up sides for a baseball game, when a large SUV careened off the road, crashed through the chain-link fence, and hit them. One of the injuries he sustained was a broken arm that they are currently putting in a cast, so we need to wait until they finish that before we can see him."

A half-hour later, they are informed that a room became available and that Billy will be moving into it, which should take about twenty minutes. When he is settled in, they will come and let us know, and then we will be able go to his room, so right now, we need to wait. Finally, twenty minutes later, which seems like an eternity, someone informs Jake and Mary that they can go up to room 238 to see Billy.

They can't seem to get there fast enough. Once there, Jake starts questioning Billy. "How are you doing? Are you in any pain? Please tell me exactly what happened?"

Billy explains, "There's not too much to tell. Like I said, we were choosing up sides for a baseball game, and the next thing I knew there was this big, black car coming at us, and then the next thing I knew I was in the ambulance on my way to the hospital."

"Oh my God! Thank God no one was killed. You guys were really lucky. Do you know if anybody got the license number or if the police know anything?"

"I don't know, Dad. Like I said, it all happened so fast.

The next thing I knew I was in the ambulance."

"Okay, I will check with the police, but the most important thing is that you're okay, and we need to take things one step at a time. Hopefully, this thing with your legs is just temporary, but to know for sure, we are going to have to wait for the results of the MRI and hear what the doctor has to say. That won't be until tomorrow morning, so let's just wait for that. I will be going home and coming back tomorrow, but your mother will be sleeping here tonight."

The next morning, at 8 AM sharp, two aids come into the room to take Billy for his MRI, and again, Mary is forced to wait. It's three hours before they bring Billy back to his room.

She asks him, "How did it go?"

He answers, "Okay, I guess. No big deal. I just had to lie still for a while."

"Okay, that's good. So now I guess we just have to wait for the doctor to look at the results and get back to us."

It's 4:30 PM before the doctor comes to the room. "Mrs. Johnson, I'm Dr. Philips, and I want to talk to you about Billy's MRI. Is Mr. Johnson here?"

"Not right now. He should be here a little later."

"Would you prefer I wait until he's here to speak to the two of you?"

"That's okay, Doctor, you can speak to me, and I will tell him when he gets here."

"Okay, then can you please come with me? I want to show you something."

"Okay." Mary follows the doctor out of the room.

THE RESULTS

Doctor Phillips escorts Mary to a small lounge room and asks her to please sit. As he takes a seat next to her, she looks around, confused, and asks, "What is it that you wanted me to see, Doctor?"

"Mrs. Johnson, it really wasn't anything I wanted you to see, rather just to have a quiet place to talk, and again, Mrs. Johnson, are you sure you don't want to wait for Mr. Johnson to get here?"

"Well, now I don't know."

"Tell you what, I will help you out. I think it's best to wait for Mr. Johnson to get here to hear what I must say, so just let me know when he does get here, and then I will talk to the two of you."

"Okay, Doctor, but just to let you know, you now have me concerned, but I will let you know when he gets here."

Two hours later, Jake gets there, and after he greets his son and asks him how he is doing, Mary informs him, "Dr. Philips is in and wants to talk to the two of us, so I need to let him know that you are here." She goes and tells the nurse that Jake is here and to let Dr. Philips know.

Ten minutes later, Dr. Philips comes to the room and introduces himself. "Mr. Johnson, I'm Dr. Philips. How are you?"

"Fine."

"Mr. Johnson, if you don't mind, I would like you and Mrs. Johnson to follow me to the lounge area so that we can talk."

"Okay, Doctor, lead the way."

All three head to the lounge area. When they get there, the doctor asks them to please have a seat.

"First off, I felt that it would be better if we did not talk in front of Billy, because I'm afraid I have some bad news for the two of you. I am extremely sorry, but there's no other way to tell you, so I will give it to you straight, and please believe me when I say that I hate this part of my job with every bone in my body, but I do not have a choice. It's part of my job, and just to let you know, there is some good news also. It's not all bad."

Dr. Philips pauses for several seconds while fighting back his emotions. "I examined Billy's MRI and also collaborated with two of my colleagues in regards to Billy's injuries. It appears that Billy's spine was actually broken in two. The good news is that under the circumstances, he was lucky that most of the spinal cord stayed intact and that his injuries are only affecting his legs. At this time, my colleagues and I do not know of any surgery that can correct it. Believe it or not, he's actually lucky that he can still move his upper torso, including his arms, neck, and head, but unfortunately, right now, it looks like he will be needing a wheelchair to get around. I know it's hard to hear that, but just think of the alternative. After what happened to him, you are lucky to still have him around."

Mary just stares at the doctor, not saying a word as tears start to roll down her face. Still staring at the doctor, in a state of shock, Jake also starts to tear up. Neither says a word, but just starts crying. Dr. Philips, seeing this, is having a hard time himself.

Mary stands up and starts to shout, "No! No! No!" while banging on the wall. "This can't be happening! It can't."

Jake grabs his wife to try and console and comfort her while crying himself and trying to say to the doctor, "Are you absolutely sure of your findings, Doctor?"

"I'm afraid so. That is why I consulted with two of my colleagues before I decided to talk to you. I know this is a lot to take in, but believe me, it's not the end of the world. Like I said, you are lucky to still have him with you. Just keep thinking about that. I know it's hard, but you've got to look at the bright side of this, and I cannot emphasize this too much: you still have your son, he is still alive, and that has to be of some comfort to you. Just keep thinking of that,"

Finally, after what seems like an eternity, Mary sits down in her chair, staring at the ceiling, tears still flowing.

"Doctor, I'm feeling sorrier for my son than for myself. I'm crying because this is going to come as a huge shock to him and be an extreme change of life for him. You don't understand. He loves to play sports, and his biggest dream is to become an astronaut and fly to Mars. This has been his lifelong dream ever since I can remember. His room is full of pictures of astronauts and models of rockets. If it has anything to do with space, he has it in his room, and I don't know how to tell him that he will no longer be able to play any sports and has to give up his dream of becoming an astronaut and going to Mars. How do I tell him that, Doctor? How do I tell him that? And I also feel bad for my husband, because he loves the fact that Billy is into sports just like he was when he was a young boy."

"Mrs. Johnson, again, I know this is extremely hard. If it were my son in that bed, I would not want to be in your shoes and have to tell my son about his injuries and what his future will be like. The only advice that I can give the two of you is to break it to him slowly while trying to give him hope that maybe someday something can be done so that he can fulfill his dreams, and you must instill in him to never give up hope. If you can do that, I'm sure it will give him a whole new outlook on life. If you want, after you and your husband speak to Billy, I can have a talk with him and explain to him that there are still many things he can do. I have a friend who has a camp for handicapped children, many of whom are in wheelchairs, and they still partake in many sports and activities. You would be surprised at what they are capable of doing. So, after you speak to him, if you want, I will have a talk with him and hook him up with my friend. And by the way, I hate hitting you with all of this now, but sooner or later, you are going to have to make some decisions, so later on today, one of my associates will be by to speak to you about helping your son and making your house wheelchair accessible."

"Okay, Doctor, thank you."

With that, and after deciding not to say anything to Billy right now, Jake and Mary go back to Billy's room, but as soon as they walk into the room, Billy asks them, "What did the doctor say?"

"Well, Billy, the doctor needs to check out a few more things before he can tell us exactly what's wrong with you," says Jake.

"How much time is he going to need to check me out? What's going on? I don't understand. Are you guys lying to me?"

"No, Billy, we are not lying to you. The doctor wants to check with his associates to make sure of his diagnosis of your injuries."

"Well, okay then, but right now, I need to go to the bathroom."

"Hold on. I'll get a nurse for you."

"Why do I need a nurse?"

"You need a nurse to get you a bedpan."

"What's a bedpan?"

"That's something that they put in the bed so that you can go to the bathroom."

"I don't want that. Can't you just help me get out of the bed and get to the bathroom?"

"No, I'm afraid it's not that easy. Just let me get a nurse, and we will take it from there."

"Okay, I guess."

Jake goes to the nurses' station and explains to them that his son needs to use the bathroom. The nurse replies, "I will have someone there in a minute."

"Okay, thank you."

As soon as Jake comes back into the room, a nurse follows right behind him, saying, "So, Billy, I understand you need to use the bathroom."

"Yes, I do."

"Okay, I will be right back. I need to get something."

A minute later, she returns with a wheelchair and a large plastic thing that looks like a back brace. Billy says, "That's not for me, is it?"

"As a matter of fact, yes, it is. I need to put this on you so that you don't injure yourself any further."

"I don't want that thing on me."

"Well, Billy, if you don't want to use this, then I need to get you a bedpan."

"I don't want a bedpan."

"Well, Billy, it's one or the other, or I guess you could just relieve yourself in the bed, and that might be a little uncomfortable for you."

"Okay, I guess you can put it on me, but I don't have to keep it on, do I?"

"No, Billy, you only put it on when you're going to be moving around a lot. You don't want to injure yourself any further, do you?"

"I guess not."

With that, the nurse puts the brace on Billy. Then she turns to Jake and Mary and says, "While I'm at it, I guess I can show you how to help Billy in and out of the bed and into the wheelchair and how to help him in the bathroom."

Billy shouts, "Why do you need to show them that?"

"Because, Billy, they are going to have to learn how to help you."

"Why?"

At this point, the nurse asks Billy, "Do you have a moment before needing to use the bathroom?"

He says yes, and she then turns to Jake and says, "Mr.

Johnson, can I please have a word with you."

The nurse goes out into the hallway, and Jake follows her. She turns and says to him, "Mr. Johnson, have you had a talk with Billy yet and explained to him what is going on, that he will probably spend the rest of his life in a wheelchair?"

"No, I'm afraid we didn't tell him yet."

"Well, Mr. Johnson, I am really sorry. I assumed that by now, you would have spoken with Billy already, but I need to show you how to do these things so as not to injure him any further and so that you can help him out, because he is going to need a lot of help. So, I guess, at this point, I will just show you the rest of the things on how to help him, but then I think that you should really have a talk with him."

"Yeah, I know you're right. We just could not bring ourselves to have a talk with him, but as soon as you're done with us, we will."

"And while we're at it, did Doctor Phillips's associate come to talk to you yet about setting up your house and schooling and what you need to know about Billy's injury?"

"No, not yet. But as far as Billy's schooling goes, Mary is quitting her job and will home school Billy."

"Well, she should be getting in touch with you shortly. I will see to that. And my advice to you is to make sure you listen to her and ask any questions you may have. Because of the injuries Billy has, he is going to need special care for a while before he can do some of the things by himself that I am going to show you."

"Okay, nurse."

"Great. Then let me show you how to get Billy out of

the bed and onto the wheelchair. One of the first things we need to get is what they call a great belt, or transfer belt. This is just a belt that goes around his waist that allows you to grab him with both hands and assist him from getting out of the bed and into the wheelchair. One of the most important things we will find out now, even though he cannot move his legs, is whether or not they will be able to sustain his weight. If he can do that, it would be a tremendous help in getting him in and out of bed, and also in and out of the wheelchair and onto the toilet bowl. It's these things that you need to learn how to do."

They both go back into Billy's room, and she proceeds to show Jake how to get Billy out of the bed and into the wheelchair. After putting on his brace and then the transfer belt, she grabs Billy's legs and turns him in the bed, so that his legs are hanging off the edge of the bed and asks him to slowly try to put weight on his legs. With the help of the nurse, he slowly pushes himself off the bed and puts his weight on his legs as he tries to stand. He can do that for only a few seconds, but the nurse exclaims, "That is great news! That will help you out immensely. Even if it's only for a few seconds, it's enough time to do what you need to do."

Next, she shows Jake how to put Billy in the wheelchair, then onto the toilet, then off the toilet, then back into the wheelchair, and then back into the bed.

The rest of the day goes by with Billy asking every five minutes, "When am I going to go home? How long are they going to keep me here?" Mary, trying to buy some time, explains to him every five minutes that they need to wait until the doctor gets back to them and that it's going to be at least a few days before he can go home.

Two days go by, with Billy getting used to the nurse getting him in and out of the bed and in and out of the bathroom. Finally, on the third day, Doctor Phillips's associate comes to see them to explain what they need to do to the house to make it wheelchair accessible for Billy and to let them know that once the changes to the house are made, Billy will be allowed to go home. But she explains to them that it is imperative that he keeps the brace on him so that he does not injure his spine any further. "Dr. Philips thinks that Billy needs to keep wearing it for at least three to four months, with x-rays in between to see how it's healing, because if he moves around too much without the brace, seeing that his spine is broken in two, it could damage the spinal cord more or even sever it completely, causing him to lose control of the rest of his body, and he will not be able to move at all, and I'm sure you would not want that for Billy. That is why it's extremely important that you follow all the rules."

"Okay," says Jake. "I will get right on it. Thank you."

Jake tells Mary, "You know what, babe? Seeing all we need to do, I'm going to go home right now, while you stay with Billy, and get things started."

Jake goes home and starts looking for a general contractor to do the work that needs to get done so that Billy can come home. First, he calls three of his friends who had recent work done. Two of them say that they would not recommend any of the contractors they used because they were not a hundred percent satisfied with the work the contractors did, but his third friend, John, says that he would highly recommend the company he used. "The owners name is Pete." Jake gets the phone number and gives them a call, and he sets up an appointment for them to come and give him an estimate on the work that needs to be done. Jake is happy that they are able to come out today and give him an estimate.

Two hours later, they are at the house, checking things out. They tell Mr. Johnson that they've done this before and know exactly what has to be done. One hour later, Mr. Johnson has his estimate along with an explanation of all the work that they are going to do, which is not too much. The main thing is a ramp, and then the bathroom, and tell Mr. Johnson that he is lucky that there is no second floor in the house, because that would have entailed a lot more work to be done. Mr. Johnson looks over the estimate and is okay with the price.

He asks Pete, "When will you be able to start the work?"

Pete says, "I'm a little busy right now, and I may not be able to start until next week."

Jake pleads with him to try to have him start sooner, because he would like to get his son Billy home as soon as possible, and he asks Pete, "What if I gave you a thousand dollars more? Would you be able to speed things up?"

Pete looks at Jake and asks, "How old is your son?"

Jake replies, "Twelve years old," and he explains to Pete, "He was run down, along with several other children, by a driver who did not stop and who sped off, leaving him with a broken spine. He may never be able to walk again."

Pete asks, "Mr. Johnson, what is your first name?"

"Jake."

"Okay Jake, seeing that we are now on a first-name

basis, I now consider us friends, and friends help each other out, so what I'm going to do is finish up the job I'm on tomorrow, and I will change the start date of my other jobs and be here the following day bright and early in the morning to get started so that we can bring Billy home. There will be no need for you to pay me any extra money, and the job should only take two to three days to complete."

"That's great! And where do I sign?"

Pete fills out the paperwork and tells Jake he will need a thousand-dollar deposit and the rest when the job is completed. Jake immediately gets his checkbook and writes out a check for a thousand dollars to Pete's company, and he signs the contract thinking that it it's great that Pete came right over to give him an estimate and that it's early enough for him to get back to the hospital.

When Jake gets back to the hospital, he informs his wife about what the general contractor did and that he will be starting the job in a few days. "It should take only two to three days to complete, so by the end of next week, we should have Billy home."

A week later, the work is all done, and the house is now ready for Billy to come home.

COMING HOME

The next morning, the Johnsons are up early, excited about bringing Billy home. They double-check the work that was done to make sure that the house is ready for Billy. Not wanting to mess up the kitchen, instead of having breakfast at home, they decide to stop at a diner on the way to the hospital. Still excited about bringing Billy home, they don't have much of an appetite, so they just order a buttered roll each, finish them quickly, and head over to the hospital. Once there, they quickly go to Billy's room to give him the good news that the house is ready for him and that he can come home. First, though, they stop at the nurses' station and ask to have Doctor Phillips meet with them, saying that they would like to talk to him. The two of them then go into Billy's room with big smiles on their faces.

"What are you guys so happy about?"

"Well, we are happy because we have some good news for you," says Mary.

"Good, because I could use some good news."

"Well, the good news is that the work on the house that

was needed for you is finished and you can come home."

"But what about me walking again? I still can't walk. I'm not fixed yet. I don't want to go home like this. When are they going to fix me?"

"Billy, Doctor Phillips is still trying to figure out what he needs to do for you to walk again, but until he does, you can come home. You don't want to stay in the hospital, do you?" Not knowing what else to say to him, Mary tells him, "Doctor Phillips will be here to talk to you before we go home, and you can ask him yourself about when you will be able to walk again."

Ten minutes later, Doctor Phillips comes into the room. "Good morning, Mr. and Mrs. Johnson. You guys wanted to speak with me?"

"Yes," says Mary. "Can we please speak in the hallway?"

"Sure."

Once in the hallway Doctor Phillips asks, "Okay, what do you want to speak to me about?"

"Well," says Mary, "one thing we wanted to tell you was that the renovations on the house are finished and it is now wheelchair accessible, and we wanted to know if Billy can come home."

"Absolutely. If you feel that it's ready for him, he can definitely go home."

"Okay, Doctor, that's great, but he is asking us questions that we have no answers to, and you said that before we left, you would have a talk with him."

"Yes, for sure, I can do that."

"He wants to ask you when you are going to fix him so that he can walk again, and I did not have an answer for that, so I told him to ask you when you got here."

"Okay, Mrs. Johnson, I will have a talk with him."

They all go back into Billy's room. Dr. Philips walks over to Billy's bed, grasps his hand, and shakes it, asking, "So, Billy, how are you doing? I understand that you have a few questions for me."

"Yes, Doctor, I want to know when I will be able to walk again."

"Well, Billy, that is a very hard question to answer, but first, let me ask you this. Do you want me to tell you the truth or lie to you?"

"Doctor, I want you to tell me the truth."

"Okay, Billy. As they say, I will give it to you straight. Do you understand that, and if it's bad news, will you be able to handle it?"

"Yes, Doctor."

"Okay, because, right now, we know what's wrong with you, but the truth is that right now, we don't know how to fix it. But this doesn't mean that tomorrow, or the next day, or next week, or next month, or six months from now, someone will figure out how to fix you, and Billy, I am not lying to you. I know in my heart that someone will figure out how to fix you so that you will be able to walk again. I swear to you it's only a matter of time. How much time, I don't know, but in the meantime, I want to tell you about a friend of mine who runs a program for handicapped children, and a lot of them are in wheelchairs just like you, Billy. You will be amazed at what you can do even though you are in a wheelchair. He has a basketball team that practices every day and plays once a week. They also play tennis, football, and softball. They go skiing, they go boating, they do archery, they go on trips, and they go for boat rides. You name it, and they do it, and you can join this club and enjoy all the activities that they do while you are waiting for someone to come up with the surgery that will fix you, and again, I promise you this: it will happen. You're still young, and you have plenty of time ahead of you, so I just don't want you to waste that time feeling sorry for yourself and losing out on a lot of fun. So, if you think you'd like to join, let me know. I will give your parents all the information so that they can get in touch with him, and you can take it from there. Okay, does that sound good to you?"

"I don't know, Doctor. I will think about it. I just want to walk again."

"And Billy, like I said, I promise that one day you will be walking again. Please believe me."

"Okay."

The Doctor then turns to Jake and Mary and says, "I will get the papers started so that he can get released today, and if he decides he would like to take me up on the offer, let me know, and I will give you the information so that you can get in touch with my friend."

"Okay, Doctor, thank you."

After the Doctor walks out, Billy looks at his parents and starts yelling, "I hate you, I hate you, I hate you!" while crying hysterically.

Mary and Jake both rush to his side. Mary grasps Billy's hand, squeezing and rubbing it in hers, trying to console him, asking, "What is wrong? Talk to us, Billy. What is wrong? What's bothering you?"

Billy shouts, "You lied to me!! You lied to me!! You told me that everything was going to be all right, and now the doctor is telling me that I will never walk again and that I will not be able to do all the things that I wanted to do. I just want to die!! If I can't do what I wanted to do, I just want to die!!"

"Stop talking like that. Did you not hear what the doctor said? There are a lot of things you can do, and he also said that he knows eventually they will have surgery that can fix you. All you need to do is wait awhile, and no one said that you can't do the things you want to do forever. You just can't do them now. Billy, you need to know that we love you and would not lie to you about something like this. We believe the doctor when he said that eventually there will be some kind of surgery that will help you, and remember, you are still a young man. You've still got your whole life ahead of you. Don't give up now, please. Billy, you are breaking my heart, I can't bear to see you like this. You've got to believe us and the doctor, and like he said, you've got to keep hoping and never give up hoping. Please, Billy, your father and I thought this would be a happy day, that you would be happy to come home. We had the house all fixed up so that you can get around it easily, so again, I say please give life a chance and listen to what the doctor said, and don't give up hope."

Finally, Billy starts to calm down, and he says, "Okay, I will not give up hope. So, let's get out of here. I don't want to be in this hospital one more minute."

"Great!!! We will sign the papers and take you home." With that, Mary helps Billy get dressed while they wait for the papers to release Billy.

When all the papers are signed, they leave the hospital. Jake helps Billy get in the car; all the while, Billy does not say a word. The drive home seems exceptionally long due to the fact that it's very quiet in the car, and Billy just stares out the window. Finally home, Jake helps Billy out of the car and into his wheelchair, Billy still not saying a word.

As Jake starts pushing Billy up to the house, he says, "So, Billy, what do you think about the changes to the house? Cool, right?" trying to lighten the mood that Billy is in. Billy still doesn't say a word, though, so Jake continues to push him up the ramp to the front door. By now, Mary is at the door, unlocking and opening it.

As they enter the house, Jake asks Billy, "So, what do you want to do, watch some television, eat something, or check out the rest of the house to see all the changes we made for you?"

"No, Dad, I'm tired. I just want to get in bed and get some rest."

"But it's still early afternoon, and you're tired?"

"Yes, Dad, I'm tired."

"Okay then, I will take you to your room."

"That's okay. I can do it myself."

"But you need me to help you get in bed."

"That's okay, Dad. I can do it myself. If I need help, I will let you know."

"Are you sure?"

"Yes, Dad, I'm sure."

"Okay, do it yourself if you want. What about if I just watched you?"

"No, Dad. I promise if I need you, I will call you."

"Okay, fine! Do it yourself if you want."

Billy wheels himself into his room, and it's killing Jake that Billy refused his help, but he hopes that Billy will be okay, because that would give him a boost in his morale. Jake watches Billy go to his room, and he waits and listens in case Billy calls him. Five minutes later, Mary can't take it anymore, so she goes to Billy's room and sees him lying in his bed, staring up at the ceiling. Seeing that he did it, she feels relieved, because that was one of the big things that Billy had to accomplish. She goes back into the kitchen and tells Jake that Billy is fine and that he got himself into the bed all by himself.

Jake replies, "Oh, that's great! That's a load off my mind, and that means that he may be fine going to the bathroom and taking a shower. If he can handle all those things, he will be fine. Then all we need to do is work on his morale and give him hope."

Six months go by with Billy refusing to leave the house, even though his mother and father keep reminding him of the doctor's friend who has a camp for handicapped children that Billy does not want to hear or talk about. All he does his lie in his bed all day long, staring at the ceiling. Finally, after eight months, Billy asks his mother to ask the doctor if that guy still has that camp he was talking about.

Mary is surprised and delighted to hear that, and she wants to ask him why he finally changed his mind but decides not to and to just enjoy the moment. "Oh, that's great! I will call the doctor today." She does and leaves a message asking the doctor to call her back later on that night.

When Doctor Phillips calls that evening, Mary answers it. "Hello, Doctor."

"Hello, Mrs. Johnson. How is everything going, and what can I do for you?"

"Well, Doctor, Billy finally asked me to get in touch with you and ask you about your friend who has that camp for handicapped children that you were talking about."

"Oh, yes, I remember that."

"Well, Doctor, he is now interested in the camp, and what I want to know is, does your friend still have that camp?"

"As a matter of fact, he does. His name is Lou Temple, and he will be delighted to hear that Billy is now interested in his camp, because, not too long ago, I was talking to him about Billy, and he said it's a shame that he does not want to join and hoped that he would change his mind, so I'm sure that he will be happy to hear that Billy changed his mind. I will get in touch with him and have him get in touch with you to set things up."

"Okay, thank you, Doctor."

"You're welcome. Call me anytime, and remember, if I hear of any breakthroughs that will help Billy, I will be sure to let you know."

"Thank you, Doctor."

Two days later, the phone rings at the Johnson home, and Jake answers. "Hello?"

"Hello, Mr. Johnson?"

"Yes, and who is calling?"

"My name is Lou Temple, and I run the camp that Doctor Phillips was talking to you about."

"Oh, yes, I remember that."

"So, your wife called Doctor Phillips and asked me to get in touch with you guys, because Billy changed his mind and now thinks that he would like to join my camp."

"As a matter of fact, yes, Billy did change his mind and

wants to check out your camp. So, what's the deal?"

"Well, first off, there is no charge for the camp. The camp is open five days a week for basketball and other sports, and on the weekends, we do different things depending on the weather, like boating, fishing, skiing, sightseeing, etc. We try to do different things to keep the kids interested and happy, but there are many other sports he can do, football, softball, tennis. I can hook him up with anything he wants to do if he doesn't like basketball, but on some of these things, there is sometimes a cost involved if the camp does not have the money, because the camp depends on the grants and donations we get, but most of the time, the trip is covered by the camp. Then we have parties like birthdays, holidays, trophy awards, and anything else we can think of to celebrate."

"Sounds good, but what are the trophies for?"

"Well, we give out trophies for all sorts of things, like when we go fishing, play a basketball challenge game, etc."

"That's great! I think Billy will enjoy the camp. So, what do I do next?"

"Well, next thing is to bring Billy down to the camp, introduce him to the guys, show him around, and have Billy partake in whatever is going on, and to see if Billy really wants to join, because one thing we do not want to do is to push anyone to join. And if he does want to join, then there are a few papers you need to fill out."

"Okay then, I will see you tomorrow with Billy."

"Great! We open at 10 AM and close at 5 PM. Later if there's a night game"

"I will see you then."

"Okay, talk to you later."

The next day, Jake calls work and informs them that he will be in late, that he needs to take his son somewhere. About 11 AM, Jake and Billy are at the camp. Billy has not said a word since they left the house. Every time Jake tried to talk to him, Billy just answered with a grunt.

As they enter the camp, Lou comes over to welcome them. Lou shakes hands with Jake and then extends his hand out to Billy, who sort of gives him a half-hearted shake. Lou asks Billy, "What's wrong? Is it that you don't want to be here?"

Billy just answers with a grunt.

"Well, tell you what, Billy. Why don't you hang out awhile and see what you think about it. Mr. Johnson, can I see you in my office? I need to show you something."

"Sure."

"Okay, great. Follow me." Once inside his office, Lou turns to Jake. "Mr. Johnson, may I make a suggestion?"

"Sure, but first, no need to call me Mr. Johnson. Just call me Jake."

"Okay, Jake what I suggest is that you go home and leave Billy here by himself. It seems to always work better that way."

"I can do that."

"Great. Just come back at 5 PM to pick him up. If I should need you to come back sooner, I will call you."

With that, Jake leaves the office and goes over to Billy. "Listen, I'm going to go home now. I need to do a few things, and I will be back at 5 PM to pick you up. In the meantime, try to have some fun."

Billy looks up at his father with a sad look on his face and asks, "Do you really need to go?"

Holding back tears, Jake says, "Yes, Billy I do. I need to go to work. You'll be fine. I will be back before you know it."

"Okay, I guess if you really need to go."

Jake puts his hand on Billy's head and ruffles his hair, saying, "You'll be fine." He turns and leaves, still fighting back tears.

Billy just sits there, looking at the rest of the boys playing basketball. Lou comes over and asks, "So, do you play basketball?"

"Yes, I do. Well, I used to."

"Billy, if you played once, then you still do. Right now, they are just practicing. Do you want to get in the next game?"

"Not right now. I'll just watch for now."

"Okay, Billy. If you change your mind, please let me know."

"Okay."

When practice is over and it's time to choose sides for a game, one of the other boys sees Billy still sitting there, rolls himself over, and says, "Hi, I'm Ralph. What's your name?"

"Billy."

"Hi, Billy."

"Hi, Ralph."

"So, Billy, is this your first time here?"

"Yeah."

"Oh, you are going to like it here. We have a lot of fun."

"Yeah, I see that."

"So, Billy, do you play basketball?"

"Yes."

"Oh, great! Why don't you come over, and I'll introduce you to the rest of the guys, and you can join us in a game."

"I don't know. I never played basketball in a wheelchair."

"Neither did any of us, but it's easy. You can learn in no time."

"Yeah, but you guys have different wheelchairs."

"Billy, your wheelchair is fine for now. We all started out with regular wheelchairs. Don't worry. Come on over and play some basketball."

Reluctantly, Billy goes over, Ralph introduces all the other guys, and they choose sides. Ralph picks Billy to be on his team, and before long, Billy is in the thick of it and having a great time.

Jake decides to leave work and go to the camp a little early, just in case Billy is having a hard time of it. At 4:30, he enters the camp, and to his surprise and delight, he sees Billy going full throttle in the middle of a basketball game. With a big smile on his face, Jake is overwhelmed and not able to hold back the tears. While several of them roll down his face, he thinks that he can't wait until he gets home to tell Mary how Billy did at the camp.

A few minutes later, the game is over. Billy sees his father and quickly rolls over to him with a big smile on his face, all excited, shouting, "Dad, Dad, did you see me playing? I scored six points!"

Not wanting to disappoint Billy, Jake lies and says, "Yes, I did see you score those points," and he feels that it is worth the little white lie just to see the look on Billy's face.

All the way home, Billy is so excited that he can't keep quiet, and Jake is enjoying every syllable coming out of Billy's mouth. Finally home, Jake gets the wheelchair ready for Billy. As Jake puts the wheelchair in place but before he can do anything else, Billy pulls himself out of the car and onto his wheelchair with no help. Jake is flabbergasted and happy. Now he can't wait until they get inside and to hear Billy tell his mom all that happened, knowing that it will make her very happy.

As soon as they get in the door, Billy starts shouting, "Mom! Mom! Where are you?"

Hearing Billy shouting, Mary first thinks that something is wrong. She comes running out of the bedroom where she was cleaning.

"What's wrong, Billy?"

"Nothing is wrong, Mom. I just wanted to tell you what happened today."

"Oh, okay. I thought from the way you were shouting that something was wrong."

"No, Mom, nothing is wrong. Today, I played basketball and scored six points. It was great! I had a lot of fun, and for a while there, I forgot that I was in my wheelchair. Mr. Temple was right about playing basketball while in a wheelchair. It was fun, and I can't wait until tomorrow to go back and play more basketball. It was great, Mom!"

Mary is so overwhelmed that she just starts crying uncontrollably while hugging Billy, almost toppling him, his wheelchair, and herself to the ground. If not for Jake grabbing them, they would have gone down to the floor.

Finally, Mary calms down and says, "See! We told you that life as you know it was not over, and like Mr. Temple told you, there is a lot you can do, even if you're in a wheelchair."

"Yes, I know that now, Mom."

"Oh, Billy, your father and I are so happy for you. Now that you see things differently, we are sure that you will be all right from now on."

NEW WAY OF LIFE

Three years later, things are going great. Billy is now fifteen years old and has settled into life in a wheelchair, and he's just full of life and enjoying it, doing all sorts of things that Jake and Mary never thought he was capable of doing. He is doing a lot more things than he did before he got hurt. With the camp, he goes on vacations. They go skiing, boating, and to see Broadway shows. The camp even got Billy a new wheelchair like the one used by the other boys when they play basketball. Everyone in the camp is kept busy. There is always something going on, and Billy befriended one of the boys at the camp, Ralph, and they are inseparable. If Ralph is not at the Johnsons' house, then Billy is at Ralph's house playing games on the computer. They are best friends. Things are really going great.

Then one Friday, while Billy is at camp, Mary is changing the sheets on his bed, like she does every Friday, and as she is taking off the top sheet, she notices sand in the bed. Confused, she picks up some in her hand and sort of rolls it between her fingers, trying to prove to herself that what

37

she is seeing is real. Even though she knows it's sand, she still needs to feel it to prove to herself that what she has found is real, let alone thinking of where it came from. But then she thinks that he was probably working on some sort of craft, which he often did, and that she will just ask him when she picks him up at the camp to clear up the mystery. When she picks him up, though, Billy is so excited about his day playing basketball at the camp and going on and on about it that she forgets to ask him about the sand.

For the next six months, things go well. Then one Friday, Mary starts changing Billy's sheets, and again, she sees sand in his bed. She thinks back and realizes that she never did get around to asking Billy about the sand the last time she found it, and she thinks to herself that she won't forget this time. She looks all around Billy's room to see if she can find what he was working on, but finds nothing that he would be using sand for. This time, though, she leaves a note to remind herself to ask him about the sand.

After picking up Billy at the camp, and with Billy monopolizing the talk, she again forgets to ask him about the sand, but when she gets home and sees her note to herself, she says to him, "Oh, Billy, I need to ask you a question."

"Okay, Mom. What is it?"

"Well, this morning, while I was changing the sheets on your bed, I noticed that there was sand in your bed, and I could not figure out where it came from, so my question to you is, where did it come from?"

"Oh! It's from the beach."

"The beach?"

"Yes, Mom, the beach."

"Oh, you went to the beach with the camp?"

"No, Mom."

"Then, did Ralph's father take you to the beach?"

"No, Mom."

"Okay, then explain to me how you got sand from the beach in your bed if no one took you to the beach."

"I went to the beach by myself on my bike."

"What?! You went to the beach by yourself on your bike?"

"Yes, Mom, I did."

Mary gets overwhelmed and starts crying, and not to get Billy upset, she just says, "Okay," and turns and walks away before Billy notices that she is crying. That night, when Jake gets home, she tells him, "Listen, after Billy is sleeping, I want to talk to you about him."

"Why? What's going on? Why do you want to wait until he is sleeping?"

"Because I don't want to take a chance that he could hear us."

"Well, now you've got me worried. Did the doctor call about something?"

"No."

"Then tell me what this is all about. I don't want to wait until he is sleeping. Now that you've got my attention, please tell me now."

"Okay, but I don't want to take a chance on him over-hearing us, so please work with me on this."

"Okay."

They go into the living room, sit on the couch close to one another. In a whisper, Mary tells Jake, "A few weeks ago, while changing Billy's sheets, I found sand in his bed.

At the time, I thought it might have been from something he was working on, and I meant to ask him about it, but then I forgot about it. But then this morning, I was changing his sheets, which I do every Friday, and again, I found sand in his bed. This time, I did not forget to ask about it, and when I did, he in a matter-of-fact way said, 'Oh, that's from the beach.' I asked him, 'When and how did you get to the beach?' I asked if it was with the camp, and he said no. I asked if Ralph's father took them, and he said no. So, I said, 'Well then, if you did not go with the camp or with Ralph's father, and I don't remember your father or I taking you, how did you get there?' Then, again as a matter of fact, he says, 'I went by myself on my bike.'"

Jake just sits there, staring at her. "Is this a joke?"

"No, it's not a joke."

"Well, you must know that it can't be true."

"Then let me show you something. I will be right back."

She walks away and comes right back holding a small jar in her hand. She sits down, grabs Jake's hand, opens up the jar, and pours out the sand that she saved into Jake's hand.

Jake now starts staring at the sand in his hand. He looks up at Mary and sees that her eyes are starting to tear up, and he says, "Babe, don't start that. You know what? I think that Billy is just playing a big joke on you. That is the only answer."

"You're right. That must be it. He is playing a joke on me."

"Why don't you play along with it and turn the tables on him."

"That's a great idea. I will do that the next time I find

sand in his bed, because, if it is a joke, he will do it again, and I will be ready for him."

Two weeks go by with no sand. Then, on the third week, as Mary turns back the top sheet, she sees sand. She thinks, *Good, now I've got him, and let the games begin*, but she can't seem to think of what to do next, so she decides to wait until Jake gets home to see if he has any ideas.

That night, when Jake gets home, she tells him, "We need to talk later, when Billy is asleep."

"Why, did it happen again?"

"Yes."

"Okay, when he goes to sleep, we can talk."

"Good."

Later on that night, while Billy is sleeping, the two of them go into the living room to talk. "Okay, so tell me what happened," says Jake.

"Well, this morning, when I went to change the sheets on Billy's bed, I found the sand again. I was going to start something to get back at him, like you suggested, but could not figure out what or how to, so I figured that I would just wait for you to see if you had any ideas."

"Wow! I thought that by now, he would have let it go, seeing that it upset you the last time. You know what? How about we do this. Don't say a word to him, just let him keep doing it, and eventually, if he sees that you are not responding, then I think that he will say something to you. And then you could sort of say, 'Sand? What sand? I don't know what you are talking about.' You could then explain to him that you knew that it was a joke and recite to him that old proverb that he needs to get up a lot earlier than you to fool you."

"Okay, if you think that will work, I will do it."

"Listen, babe, he's a smart kid, and I think that it's a great joke that he is pulling on you, considering the circumstances."

"Okay, I will do that."

Now it's only a week later that Mary finds sand in the bed again, and she says nothing to Billy, waiting for him to say something to her. This goes on for two months: every other Friday, it's the same thing with the sand in the bed. One Friday night, she has a talk with Jake.

"Don't you think that by now, he should have said something to me?"

"I would think so. Okay, so this is what I will do next. I will set up a camera in his room, and then, when he does say something to you, we will show him the video and explain to him that we knew all along that it was a joke."

"Okay, let's do that."

So, on Thursday, while Billy is at camp, Jake stops by the house to set up the camera, but while Mary is straightening out Billy's covers, she notices that there is sand in the bed already, and it's only Thursday, not Friday.

"Oh, he is really milking this!" Jake exclaims. "But not to worry. Let's clean out the sand and again say nothing to him, and we will do the video tonight to see what happens."

So, that night, the camera is all set up to go on automatically. The next day, while Billy is at camp, it being Friday, Mary goes to change the sheets on Billy's bed and to see if he left any sand in the bed for his mom to find. Sure enough, she finds sand and thinks to herself, *We've got him now.* She can't wait until Jake gets home and the two of them have a chance to take a look at the video to see how

Billy is doing it.

Later on that night, while Billy's asleep, they watch the video. It is ten hours long, so they fast forward it to see if and what he did to put the sand in the bed. Finally, they get to the end of the video, but all they saw was Billy sleeping all night and then getting up in the morning, getting dressed, going to the bathroom, and then getting ready to go to the camp. There was no sign of him putting sand in the bed or of him doing anything wrong. The two of them look at each other with confused looks on their faces.

Jake says, "Do you think we missed it?"

Mary answers, "I don't think so, but just in case we did, let's look at it again."

So, they do, and the results are the same: all Billy did was sleep all night.

Mary asks, "Now what?"

Jake answers, "Well, now we do it again and see if we get the same results, but do you think that we should wait until next Thursday?"

"I don't know, Jake. What do you think?"

"You know what I think? I think that we should set it up and watch it every night."

"Sounds good."

So, Jake sets up the camera, and they plan to watch it every night until they catch Billy in the act.

For the next week, all they do is watch Billy sleep, and on Friday, when Mary goes to change the sheets on Billy's bed, she finds no sand in the bed and now figures that the joke is all over. The next two weeks are good, but then, when Friday comes around, there it is, sand in the bed again. Mary is furious with Billy, and figures that enough is enough and that tonight, she will talk to Jake. She wants the two of them to confront Billy and put an end to this thing, whatever it is.

Later that day, when Jake gets home, she tells him, "Jake, we need to talk."

"Talk about what?"

"Talk about the sand I found in Billy's bed again. I'm tired of the game he is playing, and I want it to end."

"Okay, we will have a talk with him right now."

"Well, we can't right now because he is at the camp. They had a late-night game."

"So we will talk to him when we pick him up."

"We don't need to pick him up, because Ralph's father is bringing him home."

"Okay, then we will talk to him when he gets home and put an end to the game he is playing."

When Billy gets home, Jake asks him, "So, how did it go?"

Billy replies, "It went great! We won tonight, and the team we beat was the top team in the league, so it was cool that we won."

"That's great. I'm happy that you won and hope you keep on winning. But Billy, we need to have a talk."

"Okay, Dad. About what?"

"Well, before I begin, let me get your mother in here, because she also wants to be here to talk to you."

"Oh boy! Did I do something wrong?"

"Well...I don't know yet."

With that, Jake calls to Mary. "Can you get in here?"

"I'll be right there." When she gets there, she sits down next to Jake.

Billy says, "Guys! What is this all about?"

Jake says, "Well, I don't want to beat around the bush. We want you to put an end to the sand thing."

Looking confused, Billy says, "Sand? What are you talking about?"

"We are talking about the sand that you keep putting in your bed for your mother to find."

"I don't know what you guys are talking about. What sand?"

"Okay, Billy, you need to stop it now. We are done with the game. It was funny for a while, but you're stretching it out too far. It's not funny anymore."

"Mom, Dad, I swear I don't know what you guys are talking about. I am not pulling any kind of joke on you. I swear that I'm not. Please believe me," Billy says, and he and starts tearing up.

Seeing that, Mary says, "Billy, you swear that you are not trying to pull a fast one on us?"

"No, Mom, I swear."

"Okay, then explain to us: where is the sand that I find in your bed coming from?"

"Mom, I told you last time. It's from the beach."

Now Jake jumps in. "Okay, wise guy, answer me, and I will state the obvious. With you being in a wheelchair, how and when do you go to this beach that you speak of?"

"I don't really know, Dad. I guess I go there in my dreams, and I get there riding my bicycle, so I guess that's how the sand gets in my bed."

"Okay, and when you do go there? What do you do there?"

"I meet up with the rest of the guys from the camp,

and we play all sorts of games, like volley ball and football. We swim. We throw a Frisbee around. We do a lot of things."

Jake and Mary turn and look at each other, not knowing what to say. Jake then says, "Okay, when you do go there, and as you say, you go there in your dreams, how do you do all these things when it's nighttime and it's dark out?"

"No, Dad, it's not nighttime. It's always a warm and sunny day when I go there."

At this point, Jake decides to end it. "Okay, Billy, I believe you, so we'll just drop it for now."

"Okay, Dad."

Billy then goes to his room. Mary asks Jake, "Why did you end the conversation? Do you think that we got the truth from him?"

"What I think is that for now, we end it and talk to someone about it, because something is bothering me about this. I got the impression that he was telling us the truth. I know it doesn't make sense, but we need to check it out further. Tomorrow, I will call Dr. Philips and see if he can recommend someone to talk to about this, and for now, let's forget about the sand. Also, if it was a joke, I think by now, after confronting him, he would have owned up to it."

The next day, Jake calls Dr. Phillips and leaves a message with his secretary for the doctor to call him back. Later that night, Dr, Phillips calls Jake. "Mr. Johnson?"

"Yes."

"This is Dr. Phillips. You wanted to speak to me about something."

"Yes, I do, Doctor."

"I wanted to know if you could recommend a psychiatrist for my son, Billy."

"Well, the first thing I want to ask you is why do you want Billy to see a psychiatrist?"

"Well, Doctor, it's just that Billy is acting a little strange."

"Mr. Johnson, I thought Billy was doing well, going to camp every day and just enjoying life."

"He is, Doctor, but my wife and I feel that there is something missing, and we just want to make sure that he is all right."

"Well, okay, I can recommend someone to you, but I would like to know how you make out, so please get back to me, because, as far as I can see, there is absolutely nothing wrong with Billy."

"Okay, Doctor, I will get back to you on this."

"Great! Please call Doctor Tenna and set up an appointment with him. He is an excellent psychiatrist."

"Okay, Doctor, thank you very much."

"You're welcome."

Jake then calls Doctor Tenna's office and makes an appointment for Billy."

"Okay," the receptionist asks, "and how old is Billy?"

"Fifteen years old."

"Okay, how about this Tuesday at 2 PM?"

"Do you have anything later so that I would not need to take off from work?"

"How about 7 PM?"

"Yes, that would be great."

"Okay, the doctor will see you on Tuesday at 7 PM."

"Thank you."

Tuesday comes, and Jake and Billy are at the doctor's office at 6:45 PM. Jake checks in with the receptionist, and she gives him some papers to fill out. After doing so, he gives them back to her, and then the two sit and wait for the doctor to see them. Twenty minutes later, the nurse calls them in and tells them to please sit and that the doctor will be right with them. A minute later, Dr. Tenna comes in.

"Mr. Johnson?"

"Yes."

"And I guess this is Billy."

"Yes, it is."

"Okay, Mr. Johnson. Usually, before I examine a child, I like to talk to the parents first, and seeing that Billy is not a child but, in my book, a young man, I'm pretty sure that he knows why he is here, right?"

"Yes, Doctor, you are right."

"So, Mr. Johnson, would you mind if I speak to Billy alone?"

"No, Doctor."

"Okay, great! I will call you back in as soon as I'm finished with Billy."

"Okay, Doctor."

After Jake leaves, the doctor says, "So, Billy, now let me talk to you alone. Do you know why you are here?"

"Yes, Doctor."

"And what is that reason?"

"Because of the dreams I'm having."

"And what exactly are those dreams? Can you explain them to me?"

"Yes, Doctor. I dream that I get on my bike and ride

to a beach, where I meet all my friends. We swim and play sports."

"Is that it? You don't get involved in anything else?"

"No, Doctor, nothing else."

After many more questions, and a half-hour later, the doctor calls Jake back into the room. Then he asks Billy, "Would you mind waiting in the waiting room while I speak to your father?"

"No, Doctor."

"Okay, thanks. We won't be long."

After Billy leaves, Doctor Tenna turns to Mr. Johnson and says, "First off, how long has Billy been in a wheelchair, and why is he in it?"

"About three years, and it was due to him getting hit by a car."

"Okay, and why are you concerned about the dreams that Billy is having? Because I don't see anything wrong with them. In his condition, many children and young adults have dreams like this, especially if they were not born with the condition that they are in. You need to remember that his brain is filled with memories of things he did before he was put into this condition, and a lot of times, the dreams we have are based on manifestations of suppressed desires, and we process these emotions by constructing memories of them. So, what I'm saying is that the dreams that Billy is having are perfectly normal."

"Okay, Doctor, that's great to hear. I now know that he is normal, but this is why I was concerned. My wife and I thought that he was playing a joke on us."

"Oh, okay, what sort of joke did you guys think that he was playing on you?"

"Well, Doctor, Billy told you what his dreams were about, but the problem my wife and I are having, and what Billy failed to tell you, is that when he does have these dreams, and when his mother goes to change his bed-sheets, she finds sand in the bed."

Doctor Tenna just smiles, and Jake says, "I know it's funny, but this has been going on for a while now, and we confronted Billy many times about it, and he just explains it as a matter-of-fact thing, that he just went to the beach and met up with his friends and that is why there is sand in the bed. That is why we thought, and still do think, that he is playing a joke on us, but then we thought that if he was playing a joke on us, after us questioning him time after time, he would eventually fess up, but he never did, and that is why we are here, hoping that you can shed some light on the situation."

"Well, Mr. Johnson, let me put it this way. If Billy is not, as you put it, playing a joke on you guys, then the explanation for the sand in the bed is way above my pay grade, and you will probably need to talk to someone else about it. I'm sorry that I can't help you out more than I did. Personally, I think that it is a joke and you are not giving Billy enough credit. To me, he seems to be a very astute individual. For the life of me, though, I can't comprehend any other answer for the sand but that it's a joke."

"Okay, Doctor, thank you anyway. At least I know that there is nothing mentally wrong with my son."

"Mr. Johnson, the only other advice I can give you is that if you want to check it out further, there are people out there that do the type of work that you need done. They are called psychic detectives. Try calling them, and they may be able to give you the answers that you are looking for."

"Okay, Doctor. I just may do that."

Jake comes out of the room, goes over to Billy, and says, "Okay, Billy, we are out of here."

"Okay, Dad. So, what did the doctor say?"

"He said that there is nothing wrong with you."

"So, now what?"

"I don't know what's next. We need to figure something out. He did, however, say that there are people out there who do the type of work that would give us the answers that we are looking for, so maybe we could check into doing that."

"Okay."

"Billy, please tell me the truth. Are you playing a joke on us? If you are, now would be a good time to confess, because this is not funny anymore. Do you understand?"

"Yes, Dad, I do, and I swear I am not pulling a joke on you and Mom. I swear."

"Okay, Billy, I believe you."

Finally, they get home, and as soon as they walk in the door, Mary is right there to question them. "So, what did the doctor say?"

Jake says, "He said that there is nothing wrong with Billy and that the dreams that he is having are normal, something about him manifesting his suppressed thoughts. I think it's all bull, and I don't know what to think about this whole thing. Billy swears that he is not playing a joke on us. The doctor did say that there are people out there who do the kind of work that we are looking for. They are called psychic detectives."

"What?!"

"You know what? I don't think that we need to go down that road. Let's forget about it for now and see what happens. Maybe it will stop. Maybe he is playing a joke on us but can't bring himself to confess at this point."

"Okay, let's try that."

For the next few weeks, things are quiet and seem to be going well. Jake and Mary think that it was indeed a joke and that Billy finally stopped.

Just when everything seems to be going well, it happens again. Mary finds sand in Billy's bed and literally loses it, finding four-letter words that she never used before in her life. Not wanting to wait until Jake gets home, she decides to call him, and she leaves a message for him to call her back when he gets a chance.

An hour later, Jake calls Mary. "Hi, what's up?"

"Well, guess what I found in Billy's bed this morning."

"Don't tell me it was sand."

"Yes, sand. Jake, I can't do this anymore. Something needs to be done."

"Okay, calm down. We will talk about it when I get home tonight."

That night, when Jake gets home, he tells Mary, "When Billy goes to sleep, we will talk about what to do next."

Later that night, while Billy is sleeping, Jake and Mary retire into the living room to talk. Mary says, "Jake, I don't know what, but we really need to do something about this. I can't take it anymore. There must be something we can do."

"I know. What about the psychic detectives that the doctor told me about?"

Just then, the phone rings, and Jake answers it. "hello?"

"Mr. Johnson?"

"Yes, and who is this?"

"It's Doctor Phillips."

"Oh, hi, Doctor. I wasn't expecting a call from you, so that is why I sounded a little confused. It's not often I get a call from a doctor. So, what can I do for you Doctor?"

"Well, it's not what you can do for me, but rather what I can do for you."

"Okay, Doctor, you now have my attention."

"Do you remember a few years ago, when Billy was in the hospital and he was very depressed about his condition?"

"Yes, I do."

"And do you remember that to help cheer Billy up and give him some hope, I told him that some doctor, somewhere, someday, would come up with a procedure that would help him walk again?"

"Yes, I do, Doctor."

"Well, I'm calling you and several other people to tell you that day has arrived."

"What!! Are you telling me that this procedure can make Billy walk again?"

At those words, Mary jumps up out of her seat and stands next to Jake, all excited, and tries to listen to the conversation. At that point, Jake puts the phone on speaker. "Doctor, I just put the phone on speaker so that my wife can hear what you just told me, so can you please say that again so that she can hear it from you?"

"Sure. Mrs. Johnson, I just told your husband that I just found out that a doctor has come up with up procedure that will help Billy walk again."

Hearing that, Mary starts crying with joy. She sits down and cups her face in her hands and continues to cry.

The doctor says, "But before the two of you get too excited you must remember that with any surgery, there is always a risk and the potential that it will not work, but this procedure I'm talking about so far has been ninety-eight percent successful. And again, before the two of you get too excited, there are a few things I need to tell you. First off is the price. Because of the complexity of the procedure and the equipment needed to perform it, it's very expensive, and right now, the procedure costs eight hundred thousand dollars. The most important thing is that it is not covered by any insurance, and I mean any insurance, and the money would need to be paid up front. The second hitch is that at this time, this procedure can only be done in one place, and that place is in Australia, so you would need to go there to have it done."

Hearing that, Mary stops crying, and Jake says, "Oh my God. Where do they expect people to get that kind of money? You would need to be a millionaire to afford that. Doctor, with all due respect, I am now sorry that you called with this information. In one phone call, you gave me joy and hope, and then despair."

"Mr. Johnson, I'm sorry that you feel that way, but it was my duty to inform you of this new procedure for your son's sake, and by the way, I'm getting the same reaction from all the families that I called. But just to let you know, I am working on the cost to see if there is anything that I can do to lower it."

"Okay, Doctor, I appreciate you calling me, and I hope

you can do something with the cost."

"Mr. Johnson, you got it, but if you somehow do find the money for the procedure, please get back to me so that I can set it up."

"Okay, Doctor. Thank you, and by for now."

Jake sits down next to Mary, and they just stare at each other for what seems like forever. Finally, Jake says, "So, now what do we do? First off, with everything that is going on with Billy and the sand in the bed thing, do we give Billy the good news and then break his heart and tell him that we can't afford it?"

"Well, what I think is, knowing that we can't afford the procedure right now anyway, let's concentrate on the sand thing first, and while we do that, maybe we can come up with some ideas of how to get that kind of money, because, to tell you the truth, Jake, the situation with the sand in the bed is bothering me very much. The fact that Billy keeps denying it after us asking him as many times as we did, there is something about it that really bothers me, but I can't put my finger on it. But just to let you know, to me, it's weird what's going on. I don't know how you feel about it, but that's how I feel about it."

"Well, I sort of feel the same way about it."

"Okay, so that's what we'll do. Let's get in touch with the psychic detectives that the doctor told us about. I guess we could look in the phone book for them."

"You know what? Let's do it right now."

"Okay."

Jake gets the phone book, and to their amazement, they find a few places that offer the kind of service that they are looking for. They call one and set up an appointment for Saturday for the psychic detectives to come over and discuss the services that the Johnsons will need.

That Saturday, when the psychic detectives arrive, Jake and Mary explain Billy's condition to them and what is going on with him, how long it has been going on, how many times they confronted Billy about it, and also that they set up a video camera to see if Billy was playing a joke on them, which ended up showing nothing. After a few more questions, checking the sand that Mary saved and checking out Billy's room, the detectives, John and Pete, suggest that the minimum equipment that they would need to set up in Billy's room for two to three days would be a video camera, a regular camera to take pictures of the room, a machine to check the temperature and magnetic condition in the room, and lastly an ultraviolet camera. They agree on a price, and seeing that the sand is usually found on Fridays, they decide to set up everything on Wednesday afternoon so that it will be there for Wednesday and Thursday night, and they remind Mary to make sure she checks Billy's sheets on Wednesday afternoon. While they are there setting everything up, they also ask Mary what time would be a good time to come back to check the equipment on Thursday to see if it picked anything up.

"You can come back around 1 PM because, by then, I will have taken Billy to camp, and I don't pick him up until 5 PM."

"Okay, that sounds good," says John.

Wednesday comes and the psychic detectives are there setting everything up. They ask Mary if she checked Billy's sheets, and she tells them that she did and that she found no sand.

"Great!" says John. "We are all set here, and we will be back tomorrow afternoon to check all the equipment."

"Okay, thank you."

Mary settles down to her daily routine a few hours later. Jake comes home and asks her, "So, how did everything go?"

"It all went great. Everything is all set up for tonight and tomorrow night, and when I picked Billy up, and he came home, he went to his room, and he did not notice anything. So, now all we need to do is sit back and see what happens."

That night, Jake and Mary find it hard to sleep. They just keep thinking about what is going on in Billy's room and if the equipment is picking anything up, but eventually, they do fall asleep.

The next morning, when Jake is leaving for work, he checks on Billy and sees that he is sound asleep and everything looks normal. Then, when Mary gets up, she can't wait to drive Billy to camp and get back to check his room. As soon as she gets back, and before doing anything else, she goes straight to Billy's room and rips back the sheets to check for sand, but finds none.

Later that morning, the psychic detectives show up to check out the equipment. One of the first things they do is ask Mary whether she found sand in Billy's bed. She informs them that she did not find any.

"That's okay," says Pete. "Is it okay that we go to Billy's room to check the equipment anyway, because you never know; we may find something that will help us."

"Yes, you can go to Billy's room."

"Thank you."

With that, they go to Billy's room and start checking out the equipment. They are there several hours, checking everything out. Finally finished, they come out of Billy's room.

Mary asks, "Well, did you find anything?"

"We did find something," says John. "We found that about 3 AM, there was a disturbance in the magnetic field, so something did happen."

"But what?"

"We do not know, but something did happen."

"Well, now I'm confused. What does that mean?"

"It usually means that there was movement in the room."

"What?!"

"It doesn't mean that someone was moving around in the room. It just means that something happened, and again, we do not know what, because none of the other machines picked up anything. Mrs. Johnson, let me put it this way. The world that I work in is a strange one. Unless we get an actual picture of something, we never know exactly what we're seeing or what's happening. Remember, we are working in the world of the supernatural, and things there are not the same as the world we live in. All I can say is something happened at 3 AM, and again, we do not know what, but under normal circumstances, if Billy just slept quietly through the night and did not get up or move around too much, there would be no change in the magnetic field. Anyway, why don't we wait until tonight. Maybe something more definitive will show up."

"Okay, so I guess that I will see you tomorrow."

"Yes, you will, and we will be here around the same

time. Is that okay with you?"

"Yes, it is."

The next morning, things are going as they normally do: Jake leaves for work, Billy is slow getting up, he has breakfast, and then Mary drives Billy to day camp. As soon as she gets home, she goes straight to Billy's room to check and change his sheets, and with mixed emotions, she finds sand in the bed. She doesn't know whether she should be happy or sad, because, deep down, she was hoping that it was a joke and that Billy was finished with it all. Now, though, she is forced to face reality that the sand is real, and she needs to do something about it and can't wait until the psychic detectives get there to see if the machines picked up anything.

Later on that day, the psychic detectives show up. Mary explains to them that she found sand in Billy's bed that morning and is anxious to see if the machines picked anything up. With that, the detectives go to Billy's room to check out the equipment. After about an hour, they call to Mrs. Johnson and ask her to come to Billy's room.

John says, "Well, Mrs. Johnson…we checked the equipment and did find something, and please understand, Mrs. Johnson, the something we found may not be the something that you are looking for, but it is something. What we found was at 3:10 AM there was a significant change in the room temperature and magnetic field, which indicates that something did happen. If it's okay with you, we would like to speak to Billy when he gets home."

"I need to pick him up later on today. Can you come back later on tonight when my husband is home?"

"No problem. What time would be good for you?"

"How about 7 PM tonight?"

"Okay, that's good. Then we will see you and your husband tonight at 7 PM."

Later that day, Mary picks up Billy, but she says nothing to him about what the machines picked up. Then, when Jake gets home, Mary explains to him what happened, that the psychic detectives want to speak to Billy, and that they will be there at 7 PM.

At 7PM sharp, the doorbell rings. Jake goes and opens the door and welcomes in the psychic detectives. They all settle down around the kitchen table.

Jake speaks first. "So, I understand that you found something on the machines."

"Yes, we did," says John, "but like I explained to Mrs. Johnson, all it means is that something happened, but exactly what, we don't know. All we do know is that there was a change in the temperature and magnetic field of the room. That is the best information I can give you, because, in our business, very few things can be explained in a logical way. Most of it is based on theory, but what may help us is if we could speak to Billy."

"That would be fine. I will go and get him, or do you want to speak to him in his room?"

"Anywhere would be okay."

"You know what? I will bring him out here."

"That would be fine."

Jake goes to Billy's room and asks him to please come to the kitchen, telling him that there are a couple of guys that want to speak to him.

"About what, Dad?"

"Please come to the kitchen, and all of your questions

60

will be answered."

"Okay, I'll be right there, Dad."

Jake goes back to the kitchen, and in a few moments, Billy comes in. Jake introduces the psychic detectives to Billy and explains to him, "In light of all that's been going on, and between the three of us finding no answers, we felt that we needed some help, so we hired these two men, who are psychic detectives, to maybe explain what is going on. Billy, do you understand, and do you know what psychic detectives do?"

"Yes, I do, Dad."

"Well, anyway, without you being aware of it, these two men set up some machines in your room, and to make a long story short, they found that last night, there was a change in the temperature and magnetic field in the room, and they feel that something happened, and they would like to speak to you about it. Is that okay with you?"

"Yeah, sure, Dad."

"Okay, guys, do your thing."

With that, John starts questioning. "Billy, do you remember if you had any dreams last night?"

"Yes, I did. It was the same dream I usually have."

"Okay, and Billy, can you please explain that dream to us."

"Yeah, it was the same dream that I have a lot. There is this beach I go to and meet up with a lot of friends of mine, most of whom are from the day camp that I go to."

"And do you know the name of this beach or where it is?"

"No."

"And Billy, just how do you get to this beach?"

"With my bike."

"And when you get there, what do you do?"

"We play games. We go swimming."

"And what is the weather like?"

"It's a nice, sunny day."

"And how long do you stay there?"

"I don't really know."

"Okay, and Billy, how do you get home?"

"I don't remember how I get home. I just wake up in the morning in my bed."

"Okay, Billy, one last question. All the while that you are going to and playing on this beach, do you ever realize that you are not in your wheelchair?"

"No, I never think about that."

"Okay, Billy, thank you. Now I would like to speak to your parents."

"Why can't I stay here?"

"Well, that would be up to your parents."

Jake says, "That's fine at this point. He can stay."

John nods. "Well, this is what we came up with, and like we said, remember, this is all theory, but we believe that Billy somehow was able to escape his earthly bounds via astral projection. This means that he is able to will-fully leave his physical body by using his astral body and is capable of traveling throughout the universe. Billy can literally go anywhere he wants, and in his mind, he will actually be there, and when he enters this dream, to him, it is absolutely real. Did we lose you guys? Do you want me to explain it again?"

"No," says Jake. "that's okay. We got it."

"Okay."

"With that said, where do we go from here?"

"Well, Mr. Johnson, again, this is a strange world Pete and I work in, but we are constantly learning more and more about it, so if we come up with anything else, we will call you, or if anything here changes, you can always call us. Before we leave, there is one more thing I want to check. By any chance, did Billy ever have a bike?"

"Yes, he did, and in fact, he still has it. It's in the garage, hanging up on a hook."

"Oh, that's great. Can we please take a look at it?"

"Okay."

All three men go to the garage, and when they get to the bike, the one big thing all three see is that there is sand on the tires. Pete asks Jake, "Was that sand on the tires when you hung it up?"

"I don't think so. I would not have hung it up that way."

All three men look at each other and shrug. John says, "Mr. Johnson, this is what I'm talking about. When I say that we work in a strange world that defies answers, and you need to just let it ride itself out and try not to look for answers."

"Okay."

"Mr. Johnson, if you have any other questions, please get in touch with us, and we will try to get you answers, but before we leave, I have one more question for Billy."

"Okay, let's go back inside."

When they get inside, they approach Billy, and John asks, "Billy, would you mind answering one more question?"

"Okay. What is it?"

"After going to the beach, and when you get home, do you ever remember having sand on your feet?"

"Now that you mention that, I do remember some sand on my feet."

"Oh, okay. Thank you. Mr. Johnson, we will go back and analyze all the information we have, and if we come up with anything new, we will get back to you, but right now, it looks like it is what it is."

"Okay, thank you."

After they leave, Jake and Mary decide to talk to Billy. Jake says, "Listen, we are sorry that we did not let you know what was going on, but we did not know what to do next, because we kept asking you if you were playing a joke on us, and you kept saying that you were not. That left us in the dark, so that's why we did what we did. At this point, I think what we should do now is to just let it ride itself out, like the detectives said."

"Okay, Mom and Dad. I understand."

"Good. So, let's just drop the whole thing for now."

GONE

For the next two months, things are quiet, and everything is going as it should. Then it happens. The day starts out as a normal day. Jake leaves for work, and while Mary is making breakfast for Billy, she notices that he is still sleeping, so she goes to check on him. As she walks into his room, everything seems normal: Billy's wheelchair is on the side of his bed, his covers are up, as they would be if someone were in bed sleeping, except Billy is not in his bed.

At first, she can't believe her eyes, and she walks over to the bed and pats on the covers, thinking that he might be under them. She pulls back the covers altogether, and then it hits her: Billy is not in his bed. She looks all around the room, hoping to see him. Then she looks under the bed, thinking that maybe he fell out of it, but he is not there either.

Now Mary is in panic mode. Not thinking straight, she runs through the house looking for him while calling out his name. After yelling out his name and running through the house, she thinks maybe he somehow went outside, so she runs outside, looking all over for him but to no avail. Now realizing that Billy is not to be found anywhere, she is now in double panic mode. The first thing that she thinks of doing is to call her husband, Jake. She leaves a message for him to call her back ASAP. Then, having a hard time believing what's happening, she then runs back into the house to recheck it. As she is rechecking the house, the phone rings, and it's Jake.

"What's wrong, babe?"

"Billy is missing."

"What are you talking about? What do you mean he's missing?"

"That is exactly what I mean. Billy is missing. This morning, I went to his room to check on him because it was getting late, and his wheelchair was alongside his bed, but he was not in bed, or anywhere in the house. I looked all over the house, and even went outside to look, but could not find him, and I don't know what to do next."

"Okay, babe, I'm coming home. In the meantime, try calling his friends and the camp to see if somehow they know where he is. If you don't get any answers, call the police, and babe, please keep yourself together. I will be home in a few minutes."

Twenty minutes later, Jake is home. As soon as he walks in the door, the first words out of his mouth are: "Well, did you find out where he is?"

"No, I called the camp, all his friends are there, but no one has seen or heard from him, I spoke to Ralph to see if Billy had said anything to him about doing anything special, and he said no."

"Did you call the police?"

"Yes, they should be here in a few minutes."

With that said, she starts shaking and crying, looking like she is ready to pass out. Jake grabs her and helps her to the couch, telling her, "Babe, there has to be a logical explanation to this. He could not have just disappeared into thin air."

Just then, the doorbell rings. Jake answers the door, and it's the police. "Mr. Johnson?" one of the officers asks.

"Yes."

"You called about a missing person?"

"Yes, we did. Please come in."

"Thank you. So, please tell us what happened, and who are you reporting as missing?"

"The person who is missing is my sixteen-year-old son who is wheelchair bound. It doesn't make any sense, because his wheelchair is still here, and he is gone, and we don't have a clue as to where he is, and how can he be gone and his wheelchair still be here? It doesn't make any sense."

"Mr. Johnson, I understand. You need to understand that, normally, we can't list him as missing until he is missing for twenty-four hours, but under these circumstances, we can do it right away, so please give me a complete description."

"Okay. like I said, he is sixteen years old, five feet six inches tall, 170 pounds, brown hair and brown eyes."

"And do you know what he was wearing the last time you saw him?"

"He was wearing his pajamas. Babe, what color were the pajamas Billy was wearing?"

"I think he had his blue ones with some kind of white

marks on them," says Mary.

"Okay. And the last thing we need is a list of all his friends and places he would go to."

Mary, still shaking, writes down all the information that the police want.

"Thank you, Mrs. Johnson. We will set the gears in motion and give this information to the missing person's detectives."

"Okay officer but just to let you know, I have already contacted all of his friends, and no one has seen or heard from him since yesterday, okay great! Just remember, if you should hear from Billy, please get in touch with us. In the meantime, please try to stay calm and at home so that if we need you, we know where we can reach you, because going out yourself looking for Billy, from our experience, has never worked out well."

"Okay, thank you," says Jake. "We will stay home and wait to see if you come up with anything, though it will be extremely hard to do."

"Okay, Mr. Johnson, and again, from all of our experience, a lot of times, it's just a mixed communication, and when you do find Billy, you will laugh about it later on. And maybe you should call your doctor to see if he or she will prescribe something to calm the two of you down, especially your wife, because it seems that she is really having a hard time of it right now."

"Yes, I will do that. Thank you."

"We are going to leave now to get the ball rolling. We will get this information to the detectives right away so that they can get started."

As soon as the detectives get the information, they

immediately get started. The first thing they do is put out an Amber Alert. Then they go to the day camp and question everyone there, but with no results. It seems that no one there has seen or heard from Billy. Over the next few days, they start canvasing the neighborhood to see if anyone heard or saw anything, again with no results.

In the meantime, as the days pass, Mary and Jake are at their wits' end and don't know where to turn next. Then Jake gets an idea.

"I'll be right back."

"Where are you going?"

"I'm going into the garage to check out something."

"Check what?"

"I want to see if Billy's bike is there."

Once in the garage, he sees that the bike is still hanging in the same spot. When he goes back inside, Mary asks him, "Well, was the bike there?"

"Yes, it was. I thought that it couldn't hurt to check it out, because of what has been going on around here lately. And by the way, the sand that I cleaned off the tires last time, is back on the tires. You know what, babe? While we are at it, I want to check something else out. I want to call those guys, the psychic detectives, back to see if maybe they can help us understand what is going on here, because I just can't wrap my head around this. I'm thinking, and this may sound crazy, but seeing what has been going on with Billy, could it be that Billy is stuck or lost somewhere in one of his dreams?"

"You know what? That's a good idea; let's call them. At this point we have nothing to lose."

Jake calls them, fills them in on what's going on, and

they tell him that they can come over in about an hour.

"Okay, great. See you then," Jake tells them.

Sure enough, one hour later, the doorbell rings, and it's the psychic detectives.

"Hi Jake," says Pete. "So, tell me again what's going on."

"Well, last week, Billy was sleeping late. Mary went in to wake him up. His wheelchair was still there, but Billy was gone. We called the police, and they took the information and gave it to the detectives, and as of today, the detectives have no idea where Billy is. So, not knowing where to turn next, and because of Billy's past with his dreams and the sand in the bed and all, we decided to call you guys."

"Okay, tell you what. We are going to set up some equipment in Billy's room tonight, and then we'll come back tomorrow to check them out."

"Okay, sounds good," Jake says. "Can I ask you a question?"

"Yeah, sure."

"Well, I got this crazy idea. Is it possible that he's stuck or lost in one of his dreams and can't get back?"

"You know what? Like I explained to you before, in the psychic world that I work in, anything is possible, so it's not such a crazy idea that you think it is. You may be right, and in that case, I hope for his sake he can find his way home, because we would have no idea where he is. Even if we were able to send someone to get him, we would not know where to send them. So, Mr. Johnson, that idea is not as crazy as you think. Anyway, we will see you tomorrow at 12 noon, and in the meantime, we hope you hear something positive."

"Thank you. See you tomorrow."

The next day, at 12 noon sharp, the psychic detectives get there and go straight to Billy's room to check the machines. They work there for over two hours and then come out to speak to Mr. Johnson.

"We are sorry, but the machines had nothing on them. There was no sign of anything going on in Billy's room. We are sorry, but please call us if you think that we can help you out in any way."

Three weeks go by with no news about Billy's whereabouts, and Mary is practically living on tranquilizers. It's as though Billy has just vanished from the face of the earth. Then, one morning as Mary is passing Billy's room, she glances in like she has done every day for the past three weeks. She is shocked and can't believe her eyes, because there is Billy, fast asleep in his bed, as though he was never gone.

Unable to control herself, she starts yelling, "Billy, you're home! You're home! Thank God you're home!" She runs into the room, grabs Billy, and starts hugging and kissing him, crying hysterically, and waking him up.

Billy shouts, "Mom, what's going on?"

"What do you mean what's going on? You have been gone for the past three weeks. You just disappeared without letting anyone know. Even the police are looking for you. You had your father and I going out of our minds with fear, wondering what happened to you."

"Oh, that. I'm sorry, Mom. I meant to leave a note for you, but the escape window was closing, and I did not have any time. We had to blast off right away."

"Billy, what on earth are you talking about?"

"I'm talking about where I went, Mom. I went to Mars with Ralph and his father. Ralph's father knew that I always wanted to go to Mars, and he being an engineer and all, built a rocket ship, and all three of us went to Mars and had a great time there. In fact, I brought you back a souvenir."

He reaches under his pillow, brings out a small, red rock, and hands it to her. "How do you like it, Mom?"

"Ah, I love it."

"You should, Mom, because I don't think that there is any other person on earth that has one."

"I imagine so, Billy. I really love it and will make sure I put it in a safe place so as not to lose it. By the way, Billy, have you eaten anything, are you hungry?"

"Yes, I am. Can you make me some pancakes?"

"You got it."

Before making Billy's pancakes, Mary calls Jake's job and leaves a message to have him call back ASAP but also letting him know that it's not an emergency. About an hour later, Jake calls back.

"What going on?" he asks.

"Can you come home?" says Mary.

"Sure, but why? What happened now?"

"Well, your son, Billy, is home. I found him this morning sound asleep in his bed."

"What!! I'll be home as soon as I can."

"Okay, babe."

THE MYSTERY THICKENS

While Billy is eating his pancakes, Mary, being curious, goes to his room to check his sheets, and as she does, sure enough, she finds something. It's red dirt, and quite a bit of it. She gets an empty jar, scoops up the red dirt, and puts it into the jar. An hour later, Jake gets home, and after he greets, hugs, and welcomes Billy, Mary fills him in on what happened.

"So, babe, let me understand this whole thing. This morning, you find Billy in his bed, and he tells you, 'Oh yeah, I went to Mars and did not have time to leave you a note.' Then you say that he pulled a small, red rock out from under his pillow?"

"Yes, babe, that is what I'm telling you."

"And does the rock look like it came from Mars, not that I would know if it did or not."

"Well, babe, not only that, but I was curious, so I went to his room to check his sheets, and this is what I found there." Mary grabs Jake's hand and says, "Open your hand." He does, and she pours some of the red dirt into his hand.

He looks up at her and just stares at her. "Do you think that this could be real?"

"Who knows? You know what the psychic detectives said about what is going on."

"I guess what we need to do next is get these things checked out, but by who?"

"What about the psychic detectives? They had the sand checked for us last time.

"Yeah, that's a good idea. Let's call them. Can you get me their number?"

"Yes."

"Hold on, and I will get it."

After getting the number from Mary, Jake calls the psychic detectives.

John answers the phone. "Hello?"

"HI, this is Mr. Johnson. You guys were here a while ago."

"Yes, I remember, Mr. Johnson. What can I do for you?"

"I would like to know if you guys could stop by today sometime to help us out."

"Sure. What kind of help are you looking for?"

"Well…I think it would be better if I explained it to you in person."

"Oh, okay. How about 7 PM tonight?"

"That sounds good."

"Great, see you at 7."

Jake hangs up and says to his wife, "By the way, Mary, we still need to call the police and let them know that Billy is back."

He asks her for the card that the police left with their

phone number. Then he dials the number, gets the detective on the phone, and explains to him that Billy is safe and sound and back home.

The detective replies, "That's great news, but we still need to come by the house and get some information."

"Okay, thank you."

An hour later, two detectives are at the house and ask if Billy said where he was.

Jake says, "Well, he sort of don't know where he was,."

"Well I'm sorry Mr. Johnson," the detective responded, "We can't accept that answer. We put too much energy and resources into looking for Billy to accept that answer."

"Okay then, and not to be rude, why don't you ask Billy yourself, and see if you like his answer any better, because the answer he gave us made no sense," Jake answered.

"Okay then can we speak to Billy?"

"Yes I will get him for you." Jake calls Billy and asks him to come into the kitchen because the detectives want to speak him.

"So Billy, can you tell us where you were for the past three weeks?" the detective asks.

Billy says, "Sure I was on Mars."

"Billy this is serious, it's not a joke," the detective says, "So now one more time, where were you?"

"Like I said I was on Mars," Billy answeres.

Getting nowhere the detective looks at Mr. Johnson and says "Well I guess the information we need will not be forthcoming. So tell you what, I don't know where he was, but we are giving you a warning this time, if you pull a stunt like this again you could end up with a large fine, and some jail time. Okay, Mr. Johnson. Thank you very much.

We can close the case now. We are very happy that your son is back home, safe and sound. Thank you."

Finally, at 7:15 PM, John and Pete, the psychic detectives, show up, and they apologize for being late. John says, "So, Mr. Johnson, what can we help you out with?"

"Well…do you remember what you were here for last time?"

"Yes, we do. It was because Billy went missing."

"That's right. Well… guess what happened this morning, as his mother passed by his room like she does every morning—and after he had been missing for weeks, with everyone including the police looking for him because it seemed like he'd just disappeared completely off the face of this earth—well, anyway, this morning, she sees Billy fast asleep in his bed as though he had never been missing."

"What?! That's great that Billy is back home."

"Yes, it is."

"So, then what could you possibly need help with?"

"Well…after hugging and kissing Billy for about five minutes—and do you remember the last time when Billy was somehow going to the beach on his bike, and us finding sand in his bed? Well, when Mary asked Billy where he was for the past few weeks, and this may be a first for you guys, Billy calmly says, 'Oh, I went to Mars with Ralph and his father. Ralph's father knew that I always wanted to go to Mars, so he built a rocket ship for us to go to Mars. I meant to leave you a note, but the blastoff window was closing fast, and I did not have time to write one.' Then, as Mary is questioning Billy, he again calmly says, 'Oh, by the way, Mom, I brought you back a souvenir,' and with that, he reaches under his pillow and pulls out a small, red rock.

And it's not over. Later on, because Mary's curiosity got the best of her, she went to check Billy's sheets, and guess what she finds?"

"Sand?"

"No, she finds red dirt, and that is when we decided to call you guys, because the last time with the sand, you guys had it checked and actually told us where it came from. So, now we think with the red dirt and red rock, maybe you guys can get us some answers and see if they are real or not. That's why we called you guys, because, at this point, we are totally lost as to what is going on here."

"Well, okay. I guess we could take the rock and dirt and get them checked out for you, but other than that, we would not be able to explain what is going on here, because, if you remember what we told you the last time, we work in a very strange world, where logic does not exist, and there are no reasonable explanations that make any sense. But we would be more than happy to get the rock and soil checked out, for our own curiosity if not for yours."

"Okay, I would appreciate that."

And let me know if there will be a charge for your help, we will cross that bridge when we get to it.

"Great. Give us the rock and soil, and we will get them checked out and get back to you, and I will give you a receipt for them and not for anything else. Again, think of the strange world we work in, where anything can be real. If, in fact, these two things are real, they would be worth a lot of money. By the way, is Billy home, and could we talk to him?"

"Yeah, sure."

Jake goes to Billy's room and asks him to come into

the living room, saying, "The guys who were here last time want to ask you a few questions."

Billy comes into the living room and says, "Oh, hi. It's you guys again."

John says, "Yes, it is, Billy. Can we ask you a few questions?"

"Sure."

"Okay, first off, Billy you say that Ralph's father built a rocket ship, because he knew that you always wanted to go to Mars? And Billy how did he know this?"

"Ralph and I always talked about it with his father "

"How long did it take for Ralph's father to build the rocket ship?"

"I don't know"

"How long did it take you to get to Mars?"

"I don't remember."

"Well, was it right away?"

"Oh no, it took a while."

"Okay, and when you got there, did you need to wear a space suit?"

"No."

"What were you wearing?"

"My jeans and polo shirt."

"What about shoes, did you have any on?"

"No."

"So, you walked around Mars in your bare feet?"

"Yes."

"How about the weather, was it raining? Was it hot or cold?"

"It was nice."

"And what about Ralph and his father what did they do?"

"I don't remember, I think they went and did their own thing"

"So you guys did not see each other while you were on Mars"

"I don't remember, I think we did, I'm not sure"

"Okay, how long did you stay there?"

"I think about a day or two."

"And what did you do there?"

"We just explored and walked around."

"How long did it take to get home?"

"I don't remember."

"Did Ralph's father fly the rocket ship back or did you?'

"Ralph's father did"

"Okay, Billy, one last question. Why did you bring the rock back for your mother?"

"Because I felt bad that I did not leave a note for her, so I figured that I would bring back a gift for her so that she would not be mad at me."

"Okay, thank you, Billy. Mr. Johnson, can we speak to you alone."

"Sure."

They move into the kitchen. John says, "Mr. Johnson, from the answers I got from Billy, to him, he was, in fact, on Mars. You may find it hard to believe, but from all of our experience, even under hypnosis, people who experienced things like this are, in fact, really at the place that they imagine they are, wherever that may be. Anyway, we will take the rock and soil and get them checked out and get back to you with the findings."

"Okay, thank you."

"As far as I know, the only Mars rocks are meteors that

crashed into Earth, but remember, they went through the reentry process of our atmosphere and were heated up, and that may have changed their composition, so they may not be the same as what Billy brought home."

"Before we go I have one more request."

"Sure what is it?"

"Do you know if it would be possible to speak to Ralph and his father, or even just Ralph?"

"You know what? I can call him right now, they only live about five minutes away, and would be able to come right over."

"That would be great if they could do that."

Ten minutes later Ralph and his father are at the door,. Ralph is super happy to see Billy because he has not seen him in three weeks. After the two finish greeting each other Ralph's father asks, "So what did you guys want to talk to us about?"

John jumps in to make sure nothing goes wrong.

"Hi my name is John, and I just have one question for you and your son. While Billy was missing, and he doesn't remember where he was, he did remember having a dream about you, your son and Billy going on a trip. By the way just to let you know, we are psychic detectives and the Johnsons called us in to try and help them out as to where Billy may have been for three weeks We ran in to a brick wall, and the only thing we have to go on is the dream he was having, so we are just curious.

"By any chance were you or your son having any dreams about going anywhere with Billy?"

"No not me"

"What about you Ralph?"

"No not me either dad"

"Okay then, I guess we are through here, Mr. Johnson if we come up with anything we will get back to you."

A week later, the psychic detectives call the Johnsons. Mary answers, "Hello?"

"Mrs. Johnson, hi, this is John from the psychic detectives. I wanted to know if Pete and I can come over tonight to go over our findings on the dirt and rock that Billy brought back."

"Wow! You talk about it in a matter-of-fact way."

"Well, Mrs. Johnson, do you remember what we told you about the world we work in? We told you that as far as Billy's concerned, he was there, and no matter what you say to him or how you try to reason with him, you will not be able to change his mind. And can you say for certain that he did not go there? I know I can't. Well, you know what? I can explain better in person tonight if you and your husband are available."

"Yes, we are. How about 8 PM?"

"That sounds great. Pete and I will see you tonight at 8PM."

At 8 PM sharp, the doorbell rings. Jake opens the door and welcomes Pete and John in. They shake hands, and Jake escorts them into the living room and asks them to please have a seat.

John says, "Well, Mr. and Mrs. Johnson, to make a long story short, we had the rock and soil checked by a friend of ours who is a professor and teaches geology, and he also checked with a friend of his who is a mineralogist. Please keep an open mind about this. The only answer we could get from them was that they could not confirm their origin and could not tell us where they came from with any certainty. So, at this point, if you agree, we would like to have them checked out by NASA, because, if in fact they are from Mars, NASA would know because of the information they got from the Mars Rover. They should be able to compare the minerals of these samples to the minerals of the soil and rocks that the Mars rover sent back."

"Okay, I guess you can do that," says Jake.

"Great! We will take them to another friend of ours who works over at NASA. He can check them out, and when we get an answer, we will get back to you."

Several weeks go by with nothing new happening except the normal day-to-day activity of the Johnson family: Billy going to the day camp every day, Jake going to work every day, and Mary doing her household chores every day. Then, one afternoon, the phone rings. It's Pete from the psychic detectives.

"Mrs. Johnson, this is Pete. Would John and I be able to come over tonight to talk?"

"Sure. How about 8 PM?"

"That would be great. See you then."

At 8 that evening, Pete and John are at the Johnson's door. Again, Jake welcomes them in and again escorts them into the living room. They all sit, and Jake speaks first. "So, how did you guys make out?"

Pete says, "Well…Mr. Johnson, we did okay, but we have a few problems."

"What kind of problems could you have? All you needed to do was to have a rock and some dirt checked out."

"Well, this is what happened, and remember, we don't have an inside track to NASA; we only know someone who works there. So, we gave the rock and dirt to our friend over at NASA to check out, and he gave them to a friend of his, who gave them to a friend of his, and they finally got to the people at NASA who do that kind of work. They are the ones who check out all the data that the Mars Rover sends back."

"Okay, so where is the problem?"

"The problem is, when they checked out the rock and dirt, they found them to be comparable to the data of the rocks and dirt that they get back from the Mars Rover."

"And just what does that mean?"

"It means that after checking them out, they think that they are the real thing, and that is where the problem is. And remember, to get to the people that we needed to get to in order to get them checked out, we had to go through a few important people to get their permission so that we could get the rock and dirt checked out, and that is where our problem starts. In short, to cover themselves, they want to know where and how we got them, and to quote them, they said that to get these, you would need a rocket ship to get you to Mars and back again, and as far as we know, no one to date has been able to do that. So, again, the problem is, what do you want us to tell them? And remember, if we tell them the truth, this place that you call home will become a three-ring circus. They gave us one week to get back to them, or they will turn us in to the FBI, because that's how important this turned out to be."

"Well, can't we just take them back?"

"No, that option isn't even on the table. Mr. Johnson, do you have a lawyer that you can talk to?"

"Yes, but then I need to let him know what's going on,

and I don't want to do that."

"Well, maybe you can sort of run a hypothetical situation to him and try to get some sort of an answer, and by the way, I'm curious. Have you found any more sand in Billy's bed?"

"Yes, several times, but I don't ask him about it anymore."

"Well, getting back to our situation, talking to your lawyer is the only thing that I can think of out of this situation. Hopefully, he has an answer for you."

"Okay, I will call him tomorrow and get back to you guys."

The next morning, Jake is on the phone with his lawyer, giving him a story about finding something and wanting to get it appraised without the appraiser telling anyone about it. After getting an answer, he calls the psychic detectives and asks them to come over that night at 8 PM. And again, at 8 PM sharp, Pete and John are at the Johnsons' door.

After settling in, Pete asks Jake, "So, how did you make out?"

"I think pretty good, but I need to ask you a question first. Do you know why they want to know where we got the rock and dirt from?"

"No, it's just that it was logged into their computer, and it requires some input to close. But to tell you the truth, I think that by whatever means Billy got them, they are real, and that is baffling them over at NASA, because, despite all the technology they have and all the expense they incurred sending the Rovers to Mars, they don't have anything like what Billy brought back. Why do you ask?"

"Because my lawyer gave me an idea, something called

a confidentiality agreement. If they just want to know for themselves and if they agree to sign a confidentiality agreement, then we will tell them the truth and let them decide for themselves if what we are telling them is the truth, but they can't let anyone know about it, and that would avoid what you called a three-ring circus. What do you guys think?"

"Well…I think it's worth a shot. We will go and talk to them tomorrow and get back to you."

"Okay, that sounds good. By the way, can you tell me how much I owe you guys so far?"

"Don't worry about that right now Mr. Johnson, there are more important things that we need to attend to right now."

Two days later, Pete and John are back at the Johnsons'. Jake welcomes them in, and before they can sit, Jake asks, "So, how did you make out?"

"Well, at first, they did not want to hear anything about a confidentiality agreement, but after talking to them and finding out that what they really wanted was to own them so that they can run some tests on them because they really feel that they are the real thing, I said, 'Well, if you go for this deal, I'm sure that the Johnsons would let you do your testing on them,' and that seemed to do the trick. So, they said to find out from you guys about the testing, and if you agreed, they would go for the deal and sign the agreement."

Jake says, "Okay, that's great news. I thought that we might have opened up a can of worms when we tried to get the rock and dirt tested, and as far as I'm concerned, if they think that they are real, they can do all the testing they want. I'm good with that deal."

THE TRUTH COMES OUT

Three days later, Pete, John, Mary, and Jake are at the office of NASA with the agreement papers for them to sign. After signing the agreement, one of the NASA representatives says, "Okay, so now tell us the truth about where you got the rock and dirt from."

Pete says, "Well, before I tell you, please remain in your seat and keep an open mind."

"You got it."

"First off, keep in mind what we do for a living and that in our world, there are things going on that defy explanation."

"Okay, yes, we agree."

"Great. I will have Mr. Johnson start at the beginning. Then I will pick up the story later on."

"Okay," Jake says, "here we go. About three years ago, Billy and a few of his friends were at the school baseball field getting ready to play a game of baseball when a large SUV went out of control and ran them all down. Billy and one other boy got the worst of it, with Billy suffering a spinal cord injury and ending up confined to a wheelchair. For a long time, he was in a very depressed state of mind and did not want to do anything but stay in his room in his bed all day. That lasted about eight months. But while Billy was in the hospital, his doctor told him about a friend of his who ran a day camp for handicapped kids, with most of them in wheelchairs, and that he had a wheelchair basketball team that Billy would maybe want to join. Then, out of the blue, Billy decided that he wanted to check out the day camp and the basketball team, so I took him there, and to make a long story short, he fell in love with the whole day camp and basketball thing. He wanted to go every day, and he loved it. Then, about three years later… And now it starts to get weird."

"What do you mean gets weird?"

"Well, just keep in mind what Pete said about the kind of work he does."

"Okay, we will. Please continue."

"Well, anyway, three years later, while Billy was at the day camp, his mother went into Billy's room to change his sheets, and when she took the top sheet off, she noticed sand in his bed, and that is when it started to get weird."

"What started to get weird? And what has the sand in the bed got to do with the rock and dirt?"

"You don't get it, do you. There was sand in his bed."

"So? What about it?"

"My son is in a wheelchair. How could there be sand in his bed? You know what, just keep listening, and maybe you will eventually see the light. Anyway, the sand in the bed was happening about once a week. We spoke to Billy about it several times, and he kept telling us the same story, that he would ride his bike to the beach to meet up with his friends and play all sort of games on the beach. Then he would ride his bike home, and before you ask, yes, I did check his bike and found sand on the tires. Are you guys seeing the light yet? Are you getting the big picture yet?"

"Let me see if I got this right. Are you telling me that your son, who is wheelchair bound, rides his bike to some beach, plays all day, and then rides his bike home again, and that is why you find sand in his bed?"

"Now you got the big picture, but that's not the whole story."

"Hold on. Do you think that we are really stupid? You know what? We did you a favor checking out the rock and dirt, and now, because we show some interest in them, you come up with this fairytale story and expect us to believe it."

"You know what? I think, at this point, I will let Pete tell the rest of the story. Maybe you will believe him."

"Hold on. I don't think that I want to hear the rest of this fairytale."

"Please give us the courtesy of hearing the rest of the story before you label it as a fairytale."

"Okay, go ahead, but you guys are trying my patience."

"Great! Pete will take it from here."

With that, Pete stands up to speak. "Okay, after the Johnsons found sand in Billy's bed several times and Billy telling them the same story about the beach, at first, they thought that he was playing a joke on them, though he constantly denied it. So, not knowing where to turn next, they called us, and for your information, we are certified psychic investigators. Anyway, we set up an appointment, went to their home, and set up various machines to check if anything abnormal was going on in that room, and a camera to record it all. The first night, we got a hit on one of the machines that showed a disturbance in the magnetic field, but nothing showed up on video. On the second night, though, we got a significant reading on two of the machines. At about 3 AM, there was a significant change in the temperature and magnetic field in the room, and the next morning, Mrs. Johnson found sand in Billy's bed. In the world we work in, and in plain English, it means that something psychic happened, and as defined in the dictionary, a phenomenon is something that is not explainable by any known or natural law."

"You know what? I think we've really heard enough, and I think, at this point, I would like to rip up that agreement and report you guys to the FBI."

"Okay, but please give me the opportunity to finish explaining the rest of the story, because the rest of the story is where it gets interesting and is the part that you will really be interested in."

"Fine! Continue, but remember and keep in mind that you are pushing the limits of my patience."

"Understood. So, moving on. After explaining to the Johnsons, we left, and that was it until three months later, when we get a call from the Johnsons to please come over. When we get there, they explain to us that Billy is missing, and they have no idea where he is even after calling all his friends and the day camp. No one had seen him, and to add more mystery to everything, his wheelchair was still alongside his bed. So, we decided to set some machines up to see if we could find something that would help the Johnsons out, but the machines showed nothing, so we took them down and left, apologizing for not being of any help. Three weeks later, we get another call from the Johnsons to please come over. When we get there, they explain to us that when Mary was checking Billy's room, which she did every morning, she could not believe her eyes: there was Billy, fast asleep. She runs over to him, wakes him up, hugging and kissing him, with Billy looking all confused. Then she asked Billy, 'Where have you been?' and in a calm and matter-of-fact tone—and this is the part that I think you will be interested in—he says to her, 'Oh, I'm sorry, Mom. I meant to leave you a note but did not have time to do so, because our blastoff window was closing fast. I went to mars with Ralph and his father. Oh, and by the way, I brought you back a souvenir.' And with that, he pulls out a small, red rock from under his pillow and hands it to her. Then, later on, she found the red dirt in his sheets. So, that is the story, and no matter what you think, it's God's honest truth."

All of a sudden, it's as quiet as being in outer space. The guys from NASA are just staring at Pete, and Pete, Jake, and Mary are staring back at them. This lasts for over thirty seconds, which, in terms of silence, is a long time. Finally, the guy from NASA says, "Do you think that we are idiots, and do you think that for one second, we would believe your story?"

"Well," says Pete, "I kind of thought that you would respond like that. Frankly, if I were in your shoes, I would have acted in the same way. So, in response to your question, you checked out the rock and dirt, and look at where we are. You just signed a confidentiality agreement so that you can have the opportunity to check them out more closely. The way I look at it is that you guys are almost convinced that they are the real thing but can't for the life of you figure out how we got them, because, if somehow someone did go to Mars, you guys would have known all about it, and that is not what happened, and you know that. So then, let me ask you this: if you guys think that they are the real thing, and I think you do, then where did they come from, and what have you guys got to lose by checking them out and then worrying about where they came from later on?"

Again, there is silence in the room. Finally, the NASA guy says, "Okay, you know what? We will do that. You gave us permission to check them, so that is what we will do, and then we'll take it from there."

"Sounds like a plan."

THE DEAL IS CLOSED

Three weeks later, the phone at the Johnson's residence rings. It's past 6 PM, and Jake is already home from work, so he picks up the phone to answer it.

"Hello, is this Mr. Johnson?"

"Yes, it is, and may I ask who's calling?"

"This is Mr. Scott Bushman from NASA."

"Okay, Mr. Bushman, what can I do for you?"

"Well, Mr. Johnson, you can call me Scott. We would like to set up a meeting with you and your wife, and we can come to you if that would be more convenient."

"Actually, it would, and by the way, you can call me Jake. And Scott, could you give me a little more information as to what this is all about?"

"Well, we would rather discuss it with you in person, face to face."

"Okay then, would you mind if I had my friends John and Pete, the psychic detectives, here with us?"

"Absolutely not. You can have them there if you wish."

"Okay, and when would you like to meet up with us?"

"Well, we could actually come this evening, or if that's inconvenient for you, we could make it whenever it would be convenient."

"I didn't have anything planned for this evening, and if I can get my friends John and Pete to come over, we can do it tonight. I will try to get in touch with them. Is it possible for you to call me back in about an hour?"

"No problem, Jake. I will call you back in about a half-hour."

Jake asks Mary for the phone number for John and Pete. He dials the number, and John answers.

"Psychic detectives, John speaking."

"HI, John, this is Mr. Johnson."

"Hello, Mr. Johnson. What can I do for you?"

"Well, a couple of minutes ago, I got a call from Scott Bushman over at NASA, and he wanted to get together this evening to talk my wife and I, I asked if it would be okay if I invited you guys, and he said that would be absolutely fine. I know it's not that early, but would it be possible for you guys to come over and sit in on the conversation?"

"Absolutely. It's never too late for us. What time would you want us there?"

"Would 9 PM be too late?"

"Like I said, it's never too late for us."

"Okay, so I will make it for 9 PM. If anything changes, I will call you back."

"Great, see you at 9 PM."

Twenty minutes later, the phone rings, and Jake again answers it. It's Scott from NASA. "Hello, Jake?"

"Yes."

"How are you doing?"

"Okay. I got in touch with my friends John and Pete, and they can be at my house at 9 PM tonight. Is that okay with you guys?"

"Absolutely. We will see you at 9 PM."

"Okay, great. See you then."

At 9 PM sharp, John and Pete are at the Johnsons' door. Jake opens the door and invites them in, explaining that the guys from NASA are not there yet. They all settle down into the dining room and take seats around the table. John asks Jake, "You know what this is all about?"

"No, I asked them that when they called, but they said that they would rather discuss it in person, face to face, so that's as much as I know right now."

Just then, the doorbell rings. Jake answers the door, and it's the two guys from NASA With one other person. He invites them in, escorts them into the dining room, and asks them to have a seat at the table.

"Scott, you know who these gentlemen are."

"Pete and John, yes, I remember them."

"Yes, but I don't know who the third guy is."

Scott answers, "Oh, he is here to act as a witness."

"Okay then, we are all here. So, what is this all about?"

Scott speaks first. "Well…we tested the rock and soil, analyzed them very carefully, and I must say that we are completely confused as to how you obtained the samples. But with much scrutiny, we ran the numbers from the tests at least four times to verify the findings and found that the rock and soil, according to the analyzed information we received back from the Mars rover, are indeed from Mars. Please believe me when I say that we are being completely up front with you. Now, with that said, we would like to obtain ownership of the rock in the soil. We also realize that they are what we call virgin samples, meaning that they did not endure harsh reentry, affording us the opportunity to learn a lot more about Mars. So, in consideration for us to obtain the rock and soil, we would like to offer you one million dollars for them, but you must now sign a confidential agreement with us stating that you will not divulge any information of us meeting with you and obtaining the rock and soil."

Jake and Mary look at each other, and neither can believe what they are hearing. Then, as though rehearsed, they both say out loud, "With that money, Billy can now have his surgery!"

Pete jumps in, and says, "Hold on a minute. Mr. and Mrs. Johnson, those two things are worth a lot more than that. Do you have any idea how much it would cost NASA to send a manned mission to Mars and return with samples like these?"

Jake then turns to the two guys from Nasa and says, "I believe we could do that, but Pete just said that they are worth a lot more money. Under different circumstances, I would not take advantage of the situation, but my son's surgery alone is eight hundred thousand dollars that we will have to pay out of our pockets because no insurance company will cover it, so can you sweeten up your offer?"

The two NASA guys look at each other, and then Scott turns and looks at Mr. Johnson and says, "Okay, under the circumstances, we could go to 1.5 million, but that would be it."

"Done, but the 1.5 million would have to be tax free."

Scott looks at his partner and then looks back and Jake

and says, "Okay, we can do that. We will pay the tax also so that you end up with a clean 1.5 million dollars."

Jake says, "Where do we sign?"

Scott says, "Well, we kind of figured that you would say yes, so we brought the papers with us for you to sign, and fortunately, we did not fill in the numbers. We can do that now, and include the part that we will pay the taxes on the 1.5 million. But remember, if you sign the papers tonight, it will take about two weeks for you to get the check."

Jake looks at Mary. "What do you think?"

"That would be fine for me."

"Okay, if it's fine for my wife, it's fine for me."

Scott takes out the paperwork, makes some changes, and writes some numbers down. Then he hands the papers over to Scott and Mary for both of them to sign.

Before signing, Jake turns to John and Pete.

"You know, I had you guys here for a reason, and I am totally ignoring you. What do you think of this deal?"

John says, "Mr. Johnson, to be up front with you, you could probably have squeezed them for more money, because virgin samples, as they put it, would have cost NASA a lot more money, because, like I said, they would have had to send a manned mission to Mars or another rover to collect the samples and then have the ability to return them back to Earth. so for them to pay you 1.5 million dollars and pay tax on that, it's a steal for them."

"Okay then, I'm ready to sign the papers."

Jake turns to Mary and says, "Are you ready?"

She says, "Absolutely. Let's do this so that Billy can walk again. I always thought that there must have been a decision by a higher authority to tell Billy to bring back a souvenir for me."

After the guys from NASA, Jake and Mary sign the papers the witness they brought with them, signs the paper work also, completing the deal.

Jake and Mary decide not to let Billy know anything about this until the check clears the bank.

Just as Scott said, two weeks later, the check arrives by mail. Mary calls Jake and informs him about the arrival of the check. Jake tells Mary that he is taking the rest of the day off so that he can come home and sign the check, along with Mary, deposit it in the bank, and then pick up Billy from day camp to give him the good news. They also decide to make it a special day and take Billy out to dinner after picking him up.

Billy is surprised to see his mother and father picking him up, because, usually, it's just Mary who picks him up.

Day camp over, Billy wheels himself over to his parents.

"HI, Dad. What are you doing here? It's usually just Mom who comes to pick me up."

"Well, Billy, I am also here to pick you up, because it's a very special day."

"What kind of day?"

"Well, we are going to take you out to dinner and explain everything to you. It's a surprise."

"Oh great! I love surprises. Can you give me a hint?"

"No, you're going to have to wait until we have dinner."

"Then let's go, 'cause I'm hungry."

The three get into the car, and Jake decides to take Billy to a nice restaurant, one that he always wanted to take his family to but could not afford. Things have changed now, though, and Jake decides to go for it. Once at the restaurant, Jake asks the manager to escort them to a nice, quiet table in the corner, if he has one.

The manager replies, "I do have one. Please follow me."

Jake is happy, because the table is exactly what he asked the manager for.

Once seated, Billy says, "Okay, so what is the big surprise?"

Jake replies, "How about we order first, and then we will get to it."

"Okay, but you guys are driving me crazy."

"When we tell you what the surprise is, it will be worth the wait, I promise, so let's order first, and then we can talk."

Billy rushes through the menu to pick something and to speed things up. Finally, after what seems like an eternity to him and after the waiter takes the food order, Billy says, "Now!! Can you please tell me what the surprise is? Are we going on vacation or something?"

Jake says to Mary, "Do you want to tell him?"

Mary says, "So far, you are doing a great job, so why don't you continue."

"Well, okay. Billy, do you remember the souvenir you brought back from Mars for your mother?"

"Yes, I do. Well, you know about all the skepticism that is going on about how you got them?"

"Yes. So, what's the surprise? I know all about that."

"Well, we had the rock and soil analyzed by NASA, and it came back as real, authentic Mars rock and soil. Now, the first thing I need to ask you is this: would you mind if your mother sold the rock and soil?"

"Well, Dad, I gave it to her as a souvenir, but what she wants to do with it is her business. If she wants to sell it to make some money, that's fine with me. I would not be upset."

"Great!! That's what I wanted to hear. So, here's the surprise. Do you remember when you were in the hospital and Dr. Philips spoke to you about how, someday, some doctor or someone would come up with the surgery that would enable you to walk again?"

"Yes, I remember, Dad, and just to let you know, you're getting me excited."

As Jake tells Billy about getting the surgery, tears start flowing down the boy's face.

"Well, Billy…you can officially get as excited as you possibly can get, because a while ago, Dr. Philips called us and informed us that a surgeon in Australia has perfected a surgery that would possibly allow you to walk again. We did not tell you then because the cost of the surgery was way more than we could afford even if we sold our house, but because the rock and the soil that you brought back from mars are real, NASA wants them to analyze and run tests on them, and they offered your mother and I 1.5 million dollars tax free. Your mother and I agreed, and today, we got the check, so now, with that money, we can take you to Australia to have the surgery and possibly have you walking again."

By now, all three have tears flowing. Billy is finding it hard to come up with the words to explain how happy he is. He stops and looks at his father.

"Dad, you're not lying to me or anything like that, are

you? This is not a joke, is it?"

"No, Billy, I would never ever do something like that to you. Tomorrow, I'll call Dr. Philips, so that he can get things started, and set up an appointment for us to see the Dr. Grubbs in Australia ASAP. Then I'll purchase the tickets and get this thing going."

The next day, Jake is on the phone, getting in touch with Dr. Philips. The nurse tells Mr. Johnson that she will have the doctor call him back as soon as possible. Later on that day, Dr. Phillips returns Jake's call.

"Hello, Mr. Johnson?"

"Yes, hi."

"This is Dr. Philips, calling you back."

"Thank you, and how are you doing?"

"Doctor, I'm doing fine. What can I do for you, Mr. Johnson?"

"Well, Doctor, a while ago, you called me regarding my son, Billy, about the possibility of a new surgery that will help him walk again. Do you recall that phone conversation?"

"Yes, I do."

"Well, I will not explain how, but I came into some money, enough to cover the cost of the surgery for Billy."

"Oh, that's great!! And by the way, I have great news for you in that regard. If you recall, when I called you, the cost for the surgery was about eight hundred thousand dollars, but it's been a while now, and the doctor has done a few surgeries—and by the way, may I add that they all were a hundred percent successful—and because of those surgeries, the cost has come down to five hundred thousand dollars. So, if you were working on the assumption that it was eight hundred thousand dollars, then you will be very happy to hear that, because you will be saving three hundred thousand dollars."

"Well, Doctor, that is not good news; it is great news!!"

"Okay, then, I will set it up for you, and how soon do you want to get this done?"

"How about ASAP?"

"Okay, I will give the doctor a call tomorrow. By the way, the doctor who will be doing the surgery is Dr. Phil Grubbs. As soon as I get it set up, I will give you a call, but as far as you are concerned, you can go at any time, right?"

"That's right, Doctor, any time."

"Okay, I will set it up and get back to you."

"Thank you, Doctor."

One week later, Jake, after taking a leave of absence, and Billy and Mary are on an airplane heading to Australia with a date to see Dr. Grubbs to have Billy's surgery.

THE SURGICAL FIX

The day after arriving in Australia, Billy has an appointment to see Dr. Grubbs. The doctor sits down with Billy and his parents and explains to them that he got all the paperwork from Dr. Philips and that he is confident that he can have Billy walking again after the surgery, along with some rehabilitation. He explains to Billy and his parents that it's not going to be an overnight cure, that after the surgery, Billy will need to have rehabilitation for an undetermined amount of time. It will all depend on how Billy is doing and how hard he is willing to work at it, but the doctor also explains that if the surgery is a success, Billy will walk again—but again, how soon that will be will be determined by Billy. He asks if they have any questions, and all three say no.

Then Jake says, "I do have one. How long will the surgery take?"

Dr. Grubbs explains that the surgery takes six hours, but he reiterates that all of the surgeries like this one that he has done so far have been one hundred percent successful.

Billy says, "I don't know about you, Mom and Dad, but I'm ready for this."

Jake says to the doctor, "Well, if Billy says he is ready, we are ready also. So, Doctor, you can set up the surgery as soon as you see fit."

"Okay, I will schedule you for surgery in two days. By the way, I don't know if you can afford it, but I would suggest you remain here in Australia for Billy's rehabilitation. That way I can keep an eye on him."

Jake replies, "No problem, Doctor, we can do that."

"Okay then. Billy, I will see you here in two days. Be here at about 7 AM. I like to get an early start on things."

"Okay, Doctor, you got it. We will see you in two days."

Two days later, 7AM sharp, Billy and his parents arrive at Dr. Grubbs's office. Jake and Mary are nervous, but Billy is all excited, because, in his head, all he can think about is walking and running and playing sports again and, most of all, becoming an astronaut and flying to Mars.

They sit for a while, and then Dr. Grubbs comes in, along with a nurse.

"Good morning, everyone. So, Billy, how are you doing? Are you ready for this?"

"Yes, I am, Doctor."

"Well, then, what do you say we get started?"

"Okay, Doctor, great!"

"Billy, please follow the nurse. She will get you all set up for the surgery."

Billy follows the nurse into a room with a lot of machines and a bed. She explains to him that he needs to change into a hospital gown and get in bed, because she will give him a shot to relax him and he will fall asleep, and when he wakes up, the surgery will be all over.

In the meantime, Jake and Mary start the long wait for the surgery to be over. Four hours go by, and then Dr. Grubbs comes into the waiting room. Jake and Mary jump up and rush to meet him. Mary blurts out, "Is it over?"

"Oh no, I'm just taking a break, but so far, everything is going well, just as expected. Because the surgery is so intense, I like to take a break so that I don't get tired and also to let the parents know that all is going well."

"Thank you, Doctor, we appreciate that."

"The surgery should be done in about two more hours. Then give us about a half-hour more to get Billy set up in the room. Then you can go visit him."

"Okay, thank you, Doctor."

It's three hours later when they come to get Jake and Mary to escort them to Billy's room. Once they get there, they find Billy fast asleep and in a full body cast just like the one that they remember seeing him in when he first got hurt and was in the hospital. Mary immediately starts crying, just as the nurse is walking in. Seeing Mary crying, the nurse explains to them that the cast is only temporary. "It's to keep Billy still so that he doesn't undo what the doctor did in surgery. Billy will need to keep it on for at least three days." Her explanation calms Mary and Jake down.

It is now three months into Billy's rehabilitation, and he is doing great. Today, he took his first few steps without the aid of a walker. Dr. Grubbs explains to the Johnsons that if Billy keeps up with the pace that he's at, within three more months, Billy will be running again. Mary starts tearing up, but this time, it's for the joy she is feeling. Without realizing what she is doing, overcome with joy, she grabs Dr. Grubbs and gives him a big hug, repeating, "Thank you, thank you, thank you," with Dr. Grubbs answering, "You're welcome, you're welcome, you're welcome."

It is now eight months later, two months more than what Dr. Grubbs had anticipated for Billy to be running, and just as he predicted, Billy is running and playing basketball and baseball, and it's as though he was never injured and in a wheelchair. At this point, Jake and Mary start making plans to go home. They are a little sad because, in the months that they were here in Australia, they made friends with several people, and Billy also made friends. They will exchange phone numbers and vow to keep in touch with each other.

Then, as all good things must come to an end, Jake, Mary, and Billy board the plane to fly home. Once home, one of the first things Billy wants to do is go to the day camp and visit with all his friends. After spending several hours there with all of his friends, who are still in wheelchairs, he starts to feel a little guilty that he is able to walk and run, because he remembers when he was one of them. He explains his feelings to his friends, but they all tell him that they are extremely happy that he was able to get the surgery to enable him to walk again and not to feel bad for them. This makes Billy feel a little better.

With Billy's mother waiting outside to pick them up, Billy says goodbye to his friends and starts heading for the door. Just as he gets to the door, Lou Temple, the guy who runs the day camp, grabs Billy's arm.

"Billy I have an idea. Seeing how you are feeling the way you are, about your friends still being in wheelchairs, how would you like to work here, because I could definitely use an assistant."

Billy looks at Lou for a few seconds. Then he turns and looks at his friends in wheelchairs.

"You know what, Mr. Temple? I think I would like that."

"That's great, Billy! But please remember I can't pay you much."

"Mr. Temple, you will not have to pay me. I will be more than happy to donate my time."

"Well, I guess then we have a deal."

"Yes, we do, Mr. Temple. I will come here every day and help you out as much as I can."

"Okay. Then, I will see you tomorrow."

With that, Billy waves to his friends and goes out to his mother, who will drive him home. Getting into the car, Billy is all excited about being Mr. Temple's assistant, and he explains it all to Mary.

"Oh, that's great! I am sure that you will enjoy that, helping out your friends and all."

Once home, Billy can't wait for his father to get home to give him the good news.

This scenario goes on for several years until Billy is old enough to join the Air Force and become a pilot, which is something that he has always dreamed of doing. After completing flight training and getting his wings, Billy signs up to be an astronaut, which is another dream of his. He is accepted into the astronaut program and starts training.

Two years into the training, Billy's dream comes true: he gets the command spot on the first manned trip to Mars. After six months training for the trip, Billy is talking to one of his crew members, who says, "You know what, Captain? The rest of the crew is really excited about this trip, but you seem to be a little blasé about it. Aren't you excited about going to Mars?"

"Of course I'm excited about going to Mars, but I can understand you guys being more excited because you've never been there."

"Oh really, and you've been there?"

"As a matter of fact, yes, I have."

"Yeah, right!! Maybe in your dreams."

EPILOGUE

Billy fulfilled his dreams of being on the first manned mission to Mars. While there, he could still see the footprints of himself, Ralph and his Father, footprints left behind many years ago.

The mission Billy was on was to gather soil, rocks, and any other interesting things that NASSA wanted. The mission turned out to be a very successful one, and Billy went on to command a lot more missions to outer space.

PS.

While on Mars, Billy did not forget to bring a rock back home for his mother, and by the way, Mary never found any more sand in Billy's bed. And no, she did not sell the second rock!

THE END

The author, Barney Alesi, is a man of many hats. He retired as foreman after working thirty-three years in the Department of Public Works, Town of Islip, N.Y. He has been married to his wife, Rose, for the past sixty  years. Together, they share four children, six grandchildren, and three great-grandchildren. In 2004, he appeared along with his wife on a reality show on Fox for eight weeks called The Complex: Malibu. He is a private pilot, rides a Harley-Davidson motorcycle, likes ultimate fighting, and played drums in a band for over twenty years, with the most recent band being called The Cousins Three. In addition, he likes to sing karaoke. Along with his wife, he enjoys camping in their trailer. He has been told that he has hands of gold because he can build or fix just about anything. He loves all children and is very passionate toward them, and his family and friends agree that he is an all-around nice guy who would offer a hand to anyone who needed help.

What prompted the author to write this book was the fact that he had trouble sleeping, and every night, his brain would not shut down, causing his mind to wander all over the place, thinking of different things. Then one night he had a dream of going to Mars, and being a pilot, he always thought that if he was younger, he would try to become an astronaut. That dream stuck with him, so it was always on his mind. One night while looking at the news, he saw and heard a story about a young man whose dreams were shattered when he got hit by a car with a drunk driver at the controls, and ended up in a wheelchair for the rest of his life. Then one thing led to another. Barney's Mars dream and the young man that was hit by that car sort of got mixed together and Barney came up with this story one night while he was not sleeping again.